Acclaim of ED McBAIN!

"McBain is so good he ought to be arrested."
Publishers Weekly

"The best crime writer in the business."
—*Houston Post*

"The author delivers the goods: wired action scenes, dialogue that breathes, characters with hearts and characters that eat those hearts, and glints of unforgiving humor…Ed McBain owns this turf."
—*New York Times Book Review*

"You'll be engrossed by McBain's fast, lean prose."
—*Chicago Tribune*

"McBain has a great approach, great attitude, terrific style, strong plots, excellent dialogue, sense of place, and sense of reality."
—*Elmore Leonard*

"McBain is a top pro, at the top of his game."
—*Los Angeles Daily News*

"A virtuoso."
—*London Guardian*

"McBain…can stop you dead in your tracks with a line of dialogue."
—*Cleveland Plain Dealer*

"What is it?" she asked. She was holding her glass tightly, and her knuckles were white, the skin pulled taut against the bone.

"Del's dead," I said quickly.

It was almost as if I'd hit her in the stomach. She closed her eyes tightly.

Then, as if she'd finally gripped her insides together, she looked up and asked, "How?"

"Three bullets in his head. I found him this morning when I..."

"Who?"

"I don't know. The police are on it now."

I expected her to cry, or scream, or something. She just stood there, though, and said, "It takes a while to get used to it."

"Yeah."

"Especially when..." She stopped speaking, turned rapidly and filled her glass again.

"You'd better go easy," I said.

She tossed off the brandy in one gulp, then turned to fill her glass once more.

"Gail..."

"Shut up, Josh. Please shut up. Just let me do what I want to do, and shut up."

She took another fast swallow, and then began nursing the drink, sipping at it slowly, rolling the glass between her hands. There was sweat on her brow, and the duster clung to the lines of her body.

She didn't look at me. She stared at an invisible spot in the rug, rolling the glass, clinking the ice.

"I'm glad," she said at length.

"What?"

"I'm glad. I'm glad someone killed the bastard..."

OTHER HARD CASE CRIME BOOKS
BY ED McBAIN:

THE GUTTER AND THE GRAVE
SO NUDE, SO DEAD

SOME OTHER HARD CASE CRIME BOOKS
YOU WILL ENJOY:

GETTING OFF *by Lawrence Block*
QUARRY'S EX *by Max Allan Collins*
THE CONSUMMATA
by Mickey Spillane and Max Allan Collins
CHOKE HOLD *by Christa Faust*
THE COMEDY IS FINISHED *by Donald E. Westlake*
BLOOD ON THE MINK *by Robert Silverberg*
FALSE NEGATIVE *by Joseph Koenig*
THE TWENTY-YEAR DEATH *by Ariel S. Winter*
THE COCKTAIL WAITRESS *by James M. Cain*
SEDUCTION OF THE INNOCENT *by Max Allan Collins*
WEB OF THE CITY *by Harlan Ellison*
JOYLAND *by Stephen King*
THE SECRET LIVES OF MARRIED WOMEN
by Elissa Wald
ODDS ON *by Michael Crichton writing as John Lange*
THE WRONG QUARRY *by Max Allan Collins*
BORDERLINE *by Lawrence Block*
BRAINQUAKE *by Samuel Fuller*
EASY DEATH *by Daniel Boyd*
QUARRY'S CHOICE *by Max Allan Collins*
THIEVES FALL OUT *by Gore Vidal*

CUT ME IN

by **Ed McBain**

A HARD CASE CRIME NOVEL

A HARD CASE CRIME BOOK

(HCC-122)

First Hard Case Crime edition: January 2016

Published by

Titan Books
A division of Titan Publishing Group Ltd
144 Southwark Street
London SE1 0UP

in collaboration with Winterfall LLC

Print edition ISBN 978-1-78329-445-9
E-book ISBN 978-1-78329-362-9

Design direction by Max Phillips
www.maxphillips.net

Typeset by Swordsmith Productions

The name "Hard Case Crime" and the Hard Case Crime logo are trademarks of Winterfall LLC. Hard Case Crime books are selected and edited by Charles Ardai.

Printed in the United States of America

Visit us on the web at www.HardCaseCrime.com

The new ones, the old ones, they're all now dedicated to the love of my life—my wife, Dragica.

CUT ME IN

I.

The girl was sitting at the kitchen table in a bra and half-slip, casually puffing on a cigarette. I propped myself up in bed, looking out past the living room and through the half-open kitchen door. A cup of coffee rested before her on the table, the steam rising from it lazily. Her legs were crossed, and she wore high heels with ankle straps. Nylon stockings were stretched taut against the curve of her leg, and I wondered why any girl in her right mind would wear stockings in this kind of weather. I also wondered who she was.

I didn't really give a damn, you understand, because the buzz saw inside my skull and the decaying caterpillar in my mouth told me there'd be plenty I wouldn't remember about last night. But it seemed to me that a gentleman upon rising should at least know who was sitting at his kitchen table enjoying a cup of coffee and a cigarette. I swung my legs over the side of the bed, and the buzz saw went to work on another cord of wood. I tried to spit out the caterpillar, and gave that up when I discovered it was only my tongue. The window was wide open, but there was no breeze. It was going to be another scorcher just like yesterday. I almost wished the damned Stewart deal hadn't come up to cancel my vacation. But then I thought of the money involved in the deal and I forgot all about vacations and heat. I found a rumpled potato sack thrown over one of the chairs, discovered it had legs and cuffs, and put it on.

I was walking out into the living room, tightening the belt around my waist, when the girl spoke.

"That you, Josh?"

"Why, yes," I answered. "That you?"

"I'll pour you some coffee," she said.

I nodded, stopping at an end table to spear a cigarette from a container. I was in my bare feet, but the rug was thick, and I didn't mind. I got the cigarette going, and then walked into the kitchen as the girl set a steaming cup of coffee down on the table. She was tall, with blonde hair cut close to the oval of her face. Her eyes were a pale blue, with skillfully darkened lashes and lids. She wore a pale orange lipstick that accentuated her blondness and added just a touch of color to her full lips. My eyes studied her face, and the first impression I had was that she modeled. She smiled and lifted one eyebrow, glancing at the coffee cup.

"Oh," I said. "Thanks."

"I've got to be leaving soon," she said.

I tried to think of something appropriate, but I only came up with, "So soon?"

She grinned knowingly. "Gal has to earn a living, you know."

I sipped at the coffee and looked out over the rooftops. Occasionally, I glanced at the girl's face, and my eyes strayed down to the firm cones of her white bra. The girl's dress was neatly folded over one of the kitchen chairs, and I imagined she was postponing putting it on because of the heat. The clock on the wall said eight-twenty, and that meant I would have to shave and shower and dress in less than a half hour if I wanted to get to the office on time. And I did want to get there on time. I wanted to get there on time very much. If Friday had been any indication, today would really be a lulu. I wanted to be there the minute the phone started ringing. This was likely the biggest deal the agency had ever...

"...who I am, do you?"

I looked up quickly. "Huh? I'm sorry. What did you say?"

"I said you don't even remember who I am, do you?"

I grinned and opened one hand in a futile gesture. "I'm sorry, honey, but I was potted."

She smiled a warming smile. "That's all right. My name is Janice."

"Oh, yes, Janice."

"You still don't remember."

"No, I guess I don't."

"The Cockatoo? At the bar?"

"Ah, the Cockatoo," I said, nodding. "A nice bar."

"*Stardust* and Artie Shaw."

"A nice song, and a nice band."

"You were drinking Zombies," she said matter-of-factly.

"I was?"

She nodded, and the smile got bigger. "Uh-huh. After your third one, you put your hand on my knee and said, 'Baby, you and I should…' "

"I remember," I said quickly.

The girl stood up and reached over for her dress. Quickly, she ducked her head, and when she stood up straight again, the dress slid down the curves of her body. She pulled it over her hips, smoothed it, and then fluffed her hair.

"My lipstick all right?" she asked.

"Fine. Very nice."

"Well, I've got to run. Monday morning…" She sighed and shook her head. "It's been real nice, Josh. I enjoyed it."

"I guess I did, too," I said.

I walked her to the front door, and she reached up and patted my face, her hand lingering there for an instant. "Goodbye, Josh."

"Janice," I said.

I closed the door and stood staring at it for a few minutes. I shrugged. Quickly, I walked back to the kitchen and gulped down the coffee cooling in the cup. I thought about the Cam Stewart deal all the while I was showering, and I thought about it while I was shaving, too. Del Gilbert, my partner, had gone up to see the author on Friday. By this time, the deal would be cemented on that end. Not that his visit to Stewart's Connecticut home had been really essential. We'd never met the author, though, and a literary agency likes its clients to be friendly as well as profitable. And Cam Stewart was profitable, all right. Cam Stewart was the most profitable thing to come along in a good many moons. The Westerns that flowed from Stewart's pen were the hottest marketing commodity around, and even though we only had permission to handle the radio and television rights to the six published novels, that was enough. It was enough because any movie deal necessarily hinges on the TV rights, and they were snug in our happy little pocket. The Hollywood boys had been barking for the past week, and it looked as if the big deal was ready to go through at last. If we agreed to it. If we didn't, we'd simply queer it, and there wasn't a damned thing they could do. No producer is going to spend a million bucks on a movie and then discover that his potential audience can get the same thing on television for free.

Oh yes, it was very sweet.

And we'd fallen right into it, almost with no effort at all. We'd simply written to Stewart asking for permission to handle radio and television rights, telling the author we had what looked like a good opportunity for their sale. Both Del and I almost keeled over flat when Stewart's return letter arrived. It granted us sole and exclusive permission to handle the rights for which we'd asked, provided a five-hundred-dollar option was paid. We sent our check out in the next mail, and I'd have been willing to deliver it personally. Then we had a photostat made

of Stewart's letter. This was our meal ticket, and we weren't
taking a chance on it getting lost or misplaced.

I was excited, all right. I was excited as hell. The Hollywood
boys had been talking in terms of fifty thousand per picture,
two pictures a year. That's a lot of money no matter how you
fold it, and we were in a position to kill the deal unless we got
what we wanted out of it. I dressed rapidly, almost forgetting to
put on my tie. There was the faint odor of perfume in the bathroom, and I sniffed it appreciatively. It takes a lucky man to
pick a winner even when he's souped to the ears. I'd probably
have dropped dead if I'd found a dried-up old hag sitting at the
table this morning. And considering all I could remember, or
rather all I had forgotten, the likelihood was not a remote one.

I left my apartment and took the Buick from the garage
under the building. The traffic was thick, and the heat was
beginning to pour down out of the sky—a heat that stuck your
pants to the seat, and your shorts to your pants, and your skin to
your shorts. That kind of heat. Damp and sticky, like sorghum
molasses.

I sweated out a red light that took forever to change, and
then I was in the Fifth Avenue stream of traffic. I had the top
down, but that didn't help at all, and by the time I'd parked the
car in a garage on Eighth and caught a cab crosstown, I was
drenched to the skin. I took the elevator up to the twentieth
floor and walked down to our offices at the end of the hall. We
had a suite of six rooms, including a large reception room; a
general office; a consultation room; an office for Tim, our executive editor; and two private offices for Del and myself. It was a
nice layout, and it had taken us a long time to get where we
were. The Stewart deal would shove us one more notch up the
ladder, and a few more notches after that would put us in the
really big agency bracket. I closed the door to the reception

room behind me, glanced briefly at the big guy sitting on one of the couches, and then headed for the door leading to my office. Jeanette, the brunette receptionist and switchboard operator, smiled pertly as I passed her desk.

"Good morning, Mr. Blake," she said. The words hardly left her mouth when the big guy sitting on the couch leaped to his feet and started across the room after me. I didn't turn back, but I smelled writer, even from that distance. When you've been a ten-percenter long enough, you can smell a writer at a hundred paces, even if he's wearing a butcher's apron. This guy wasn't wearing a butcher's apron, though I'm sure he could have slaughtered a steer with his bare hands.

He ran around me and stopped in front of my door, clutching a briefcase to his chest. He was at least six-four, weighing all of two hundred pounds, with straight black hair that fell over his forehead. His shaggy brows matched his hair, and his nose had been skillfully rearranged by someone with big fists. He had a jaw like a pig's rump, with twice as many bristles protruding from it. He looked like a rundown bookie, or a hired killer, but I knew he was a writer.

"Mr. Blake?" he asked.

I allowed my eyes to roam toward Jeanette, the promise of quick strangulation in them. "Yes," I said slowly, "I'm Mr. Blake."

"My name is Gunnison," he said, his face erupting into a somewhat ghoulish smile. "David Gunnison."

I nodded pleasantly, waiting for him to say it.

"I'm a writer," he said.

"Oh?" I asked, interest all over my face.

"I've written a novel."

"That's nice," I said. I knew the answer to the next question before I asked it, but I'm a glutton for punishment. "Is it your first novel?"

"Why, yes."

"Well, if you'll just have a seat, Mr. Gunnison, one of our editors will be happy to talk to you."

"Oh, no!" he said, moving over and covering the door with his huge body. "I want to talk to you personally."

I allowed my glance to find Jeanette again, and this time there was arsenic and a small pinch of cyanide in it

"Well," I said, gesturing to the couch, "have a seat, won't you?" I was sure as hell not going to make him comfortable in *my* private office. I expected the phone to begin jangling at any moment, and I didn't want to be tied up with a budding Shakespeare, even if he *was* a budding Shakespeare—which was extremely doubtful. I've read a great many first novels.

"We'll have to make this short," I said apologetically. "I'm expecting some very important calls."

"We won't take a minute, Mr. Blake," he answered, un-zipping his briefcase. I watched while he reached in and pulled out what looked like forty thousand typewritten pages. He slapped the manuscript down on his briefcase with all the flourish of a magician producing a rabbit from a hat, and then nodded in self-appreciation. "Ninety-five thousand words," he said. "Is that too long?"

"No," I said, "That is, it all depends on what type of book it is."

"It's based on my life," he said, and I winced automatically. The phone rang just then, and I craned my neck toward it while Jeanette went through the ritual.

"Gilbert and Blake, good morning."

"I was born in the South, you see, and this tells all about my family, fictionalized of course, and some of the things that happened right up to the time I was twenty-one."

"Just a moment, sir, I'll see if he's in."

I watched as Jeanette plugged in and said, "Mr. Gordon on six, Mr. Kennedy."

Kennedy was Tim. I slouched back against the cushions and let out my breath.

"For example, Mr. Blake, one of my uncles was sheriff of Longduck County. Now he's told me some stories which…"

"Uh, Mr. Gunnison, I hate to interrupt you but…"

"That's quite all right, sir," he said. "I've got plenty of time. What do you want to know?"

"Well, as you know, this is Monday morning, and there are a great many things to be done. It's a little unusual to drop in without an appointment, so perhaps I could have my secretary arrange a later appointment for you, and we could sit down and discuss your novel at length then."

"Well…" he started, but I was already on my feet and walking over to the reception desk.

"Jeanette, will you ask Lydia to step outside, please?" I asked.

"She's not in yet, Mr. Blake," Jeanette said. I looked up at the clock on the wall. It was nine-thirty.

"Call her home," I said, my voice getting a little annoyed. "Find out if she's coming in."

"Yes, sir."

I turned and almost slammed into Gunnison, or whatever the hell his name was. A few pages of his manuscript fluttered to the floor and he stooped down to retrieve them. "You needn't go to any trouble on my part," he said, still smiling. "We can talk right now."

"Mr. Gunnison…"

"I know you're being considerate and all, but I really didn't have any place else to go, anyway."

"I think you misunderstood me," I said. He was beginning to really rub me the wrong way, and I was tempted to toss him out by the seat of his pants, except that his six-four gave him almost four inches on me, and this was Monday morning. If an important call came through while I was sitting here listening to this jackass rave…

"No misunderstanding at all," he said. "Just sit down, and I'll show you what I mean." He put one meaty hand on my shoulder and practically shoved me down through the bottom of the couch.

I pushed myself up and said, "Look, my good friend…"

"Listen to this," he said.

"Mr. Gunnison, can't we…"

The phone rang again, and this time I nearly leaped off the couch.

"Gilbert and Blake, good morning."

"*'The sky was a pale bowl of inverted blue china. It was early morning, and the sounds of the day were lazy and unclear, as if they'd shaken themselves from sleep and…'*"

"I'm sorry, sir, Mr. Gilbert is out of town…No, sir, I don't know when he'll return…yes, sir, I will."

Jeanette yanked the plug from its socket and I jumped off the couch. "Who was that?" I asked.

Gunnison had stopped reading and was staring at me with wide eyes.

"He…he didn't say, Mr. Blake," Jeanette stammered.

"Well, why in hell didn't you ask?"

"I…I didn't think…"

"Did you ask him if he'd speak to me?"

"N…n…no, sir."

"What the hell kind of an office is this anyway? Where the hell is Lydia? What did you mean when you told him 'I will'?"

"Sir?"

"That guy on the phone. He said something, and you said 'Yes, sir, I will.' What did he say?"

"He said, 'Will you tell him I called?'"

"Who? Who called?"

"He didn't say, sir."

"Oh, for Christ's…"

"Mr. Blake?"

I whirled and found Gunnison at my elbow again. "What is it?"

"My novel," he said. "How'd you like that part I read?"

"I didn't!" I snapped. "It was lousy. Now leave me alone, will you?"

His eyes popped wide, but I didn't stay to watch them. I turned and walked to my office, slamming the door behind me. Goddamn it, this morning was starting off fine, just fine. A strange girl in the apartment, a lunatic with a novel, a receptionist who can't get a name straight over the phone…

I sat down behind my desk and pushed a toggle on the intercom.

"Yep."

"Who's this?"

"Charlie. That you, Josh?"

"This is me. Is everybody out there?"

"Why, sure."

"All right."

I pushed another toggle, and recognized Tim's voice when it came over the speaker.

"Who called you this morning, Tim?"

"Two calls," he said. "A sale to Standard, and a pick-up at *Cosmo*."

"All right. Don't disturb me for the rest of the morning, Tim. I expect to be tied up."

"Right, Josh."

I buzzed Jeanette then, and when she came on I asked, "Did you get Lydia?"

"No, sir."

"No answer?"

"No, sir. But the switchboard operator there…"

"Yes?"

"The switchboard operator said Lydia is on her way in."

"Send her in as soon as she arrives."

"Yes, sir. And, sir…"

"What is it?"

"That man is still here."

"What man?"

"The man you were talking to. Mr. Gunnison, I believe."

"Tell him to go away."

"I did, sir. He just…"

"Tell him again. I'm busy. Don't bother me."

I clicked off and leafed through the morning mail on my desk, holding the envelopes up to the light streaming through the window, looking for checks. I found a letter with an Arizona postmark, and I recognized Frank Gorman's handwriting. Now what the hell was eating him? I started to rip open the flap of the envelope when I heard excited shouting in the reception room. I was about to buzz Jeanette to ask her what all the noise was about when the door burst open and Gunnison rushed in with his briefcase tight against his chest. Jeanette was right behind him, her face pale.

"I'm s…sorry, sir," she stammered.

"That's all right," I told her. She backed out of the office, and I shoved my chair away from the desk and walked over to Gunnison. "What the hell do you think this is?" I asked. "A gymnasium?"

"Why won't you read my book?" he said softly. His thick black brows were knotted ominously, and his lips were compressed into a tight line through which he forced out his words.

"I didn't say I wouldn't read it," I answered, beginning to get angry with the guy all over again. "I told you to make an appointment. That was before you came barging in here like Army's eleven. Now you can take your book and…"

"You're all the same," he mumbled. "All of you. Not one of you will give a new writer a break."

"All writers are new writers once," I said. "I think you'd better go."

I was turning to walk back to my chair when his hand clamped down on my shoulder. He yanked his arm back, spinning me around and grabbing my lapels up in his other hand. He gave a vicious jerk that pulled me off my feet, and then, with his face about two inches from mine, he said, "This isn't the end of this, you bastard."

I do not like being called names, and I do not like being threatened. I also do not like the lapels of my suits crushed in anybody's mitts, even if the anybody is six-four. I lifted my foot about six inches off the floor, and then brought the heel down on his instep.

He dropped my lapels, let out a yell, and then grabbed for his foot. I shoved the palm of my hand against his chest and he went flying back, butt over teacups, the briefcase jumping into the air. I reached down, grabbed the seat of his pants and the collar of his suit, and propelled him to the front door as fast as I could. He swore all the way, and he wiggled like a snake when I let go with one hand to open the door. He was ready to turn on me when I shoved him out into the hallway. His shoes hit the waxed floors and he skidded for about four feet, his arms flaying like a comic ice-skater's. He went down, then, all at once, and the building shook a little when he hit the floor.

"Don't come back," I said. "The police are only a phone call away."

"You bastard," he muttered. "You still have my book."

"I'll send it out. Goodbye, friend."

"You bastard," he said again.

I closed the door on him, walked straight to my office, and then buzzed Jeanette. When she came in, I handed her Gunnison's briefcase. "Give this to the gentleman sitting in the hallway," I told her.

She turned to go, and I said, "Has Lydia come in yet?"

"No, sir."

When she left, I picked up Frank Gorman's letter again. Frank was a mystery writer who'd been with the agency for about five years. He wrote pulps mostly, with a few scattered slick tries, but he was a steady producer, the kind of old reliable any agent likes in his stable. I tore open the envelope and pulled out the letter. It was written on yellow lined paper, the way all Frank's letters were, and it began, *"Dear Josh, I'd like to cancel our contract as of today."*

That tied it! That bloody well tied it. It was like someone's own father stabbing him. I read through the letter, getting angrier every second. I crumpled it into a ball and threw it at the bookcase across the room, missing. I buzzed Jeanette.

"Has our alleged secretary shown up yet?"

"No, sir."

"Have there been any calls?"

"No, sir."

"All right."

I got up and walked across the room to pick up Gorman's letter. I wondered when his contract expired, and then I decided to find out. I'd be goddamned if I was just going to let him walk out on us after five years of building his name and steering him along, I took out my keys and unlocked the door between my office and Del's. The safe was in Del's office, and we kept all our contracts in the safe. I put the keys back into my pocket and swung the door wide.

The first thing I saw almost caused the top of my skull to blow off because I thought it was just another glaring example of office inefficiency. The safe was open and a sheaf of papers was spilled all over the floor. I tightened my fists and barged into the office, ready to start screaming bloody murder.

Then I saw Del, and I had every right to scream just that.

2.

He was lying on the floor. In front of the couch, which was perfectly all right since this was his office, after all. But three holes had very carelessly been left in his face. Two were set close together on his forehead, and the third rested just beneath his left eye, like a small dark tunnel. His head was tilted to one side, and his mouth was open, and the rivers of blood that crisscrossed over his face formed a soggy red pool on the rug beneath his head.

There was another pool on the floor, beneath the aquarium in which Del had kept his tropical fish. The tank was empty of water now, with a few fish still wriggling on its damp bottom. The glass front had been smashed in, and I wondered idly why anyone would want to smash a fish tank.

The mind works like that sometimes. I knew Del was dead, and I knew those were bullet holes in his head, but I didn't stop to wonder who had killed him. In fact, I don't think I even realized at the moment that someone *had* killed him. I simply accepted the corpse and then wondered about the aquarium.

I took my eyes from the tank, and looked down at Del again. A sudden desire to laugh seized me, and I wondered about my own sanity. I stared at the body, looking at the blood and the holes, and then the buzzer on Del's desk sounded.

I turned my head slowly, listening to the insistent hum. I walked across the room to the desk, pushed down one of the toggles and asked, "Yes?" The hoarseness of my own voice surprised me.

"I figured you were in Mr. Gilbert's office," Jeanette said proudly. "Lydia is here, sir."

"Who?" I asked. My eyes were on Del's body.

"Lydia, sir."

"Oh. Oh, send her right in, will you?"

"Yes, si…"

"No!" I said suddenly. "No, ask her…ask her to wait outside, will you? Tell her to wait. I…I'll buzz you."

"Yes, sir." Jeanette's voice was puzzled when she clicked off.

I collapsed into the chair behind Del's long, wide desk, looking over its polished top to where Del lay bleeding on the rug. My brows were pulled together, and I looked at him the way I'd look at a modern painting I didn't understand. I let out a sigh and pushed down Tim's toggle.

"Yep?"

"Tim?"

"Yes, Josh."

"Will you come in here a minute? I'm in Del's office."

"Sure, be right there. Important?"

"Yes. Yes, Tim, it's important."

"Be right in."

I clicked off, and then leaned back to wait. After a little while, Del's front door opened, and Tim came in.

He was a tall, lanky boy with bushy black hair and deep brown eyes. Tim Kennedy, and he looked about as Irish as Sinbad the Sailor.

"What's up, Josh?" he asked. He leaned over, putting his palms flat on the desk. He still had his back to the body, and I didn't know quite how to tell him about what was lying behind him on the rug.

"What time did you get in this morning, Tim?"

"About nine." He grinned broadly, exposing teeth that were too large for his thin lips. "Another shakedown, huh? Okay, boss, let's see. I got in at nine-oh-five on the button. Jeanette was already here, and so were Charlie and Sam. Burry got in at about…"

"Did anyone come into this office?"

Tim paused and eyed me skeptically. "Here? Del's office? Why, no. Is something missing?" He turned rapidly, then, to glance automatically at the safe. I couldn't see his face because his back was to me. But his spine seemed to buckle, and he backed up several paces until he collided with the desk, and I knew he'd seen Del.

"Oh my God," he said. "Oh, sweet mother of God."

"Yeah," I said, trying to find my voice.

He turned to me, his face working, his Adam's apple moving fitfully in his throat. "When…when…"

"I just found him, Tim. Just before I buzzed you."

He took another look at the body, and then turned away quickly. He reached behind him for the chair alongside the desk, found it and pulled himself into it. He buried his face in his hands then, and I said, "I'd better call the police."

"Yes. Yes," he said.

I threw down Jeanette's toggle.

"Yes, sir?"

"Get me the police."

"Sir?"

"The police, Jeanette. Please hurry."

"Y-y-yes, sir."

I suddenly wondered why I'd asked her to hurry. Del was already dead, and nothing the police could do would bring him back to life.

"Josh," Tim said.

"Um?"

"Josh, this is…terrible. Who…who do you suppose…?"

"I have no idea, Tim."

"But why? I mean…"

The door opened then, and Lydia Rafney burst into the office like a fresh breeze into a mausoleum. She was wearing a trim linen suit, with her auburn hair pulled back in a saucy pony-tail. She was built like a best-seller, with as much of a following, and there was a bright grin on her face.

"Good morning, good morning," she started, and then her features froze. Her mouth fell open, the full, red lips parting over a small 'O'. Her eyebrows jerked up onto her forehead, and I saw terror strike deep within the greenness of her eyes.

"No!" She stared at the body and then whirled away, covering her face with her hands. Her next word was screamed. *"No!"*

I went to her and put one arm around her, and if she was faking she was a damned good actress. Her body was trembling, with deep, racking sobs that started at her toes and forced their way up into her throat.

"Josh," she whimpered, "oh, Josh, he's dead, he's dead."

It's uncomfortable to hold your secretary in your arms, especially when you know she was shacking up with your partner, and your partner has three extra holes in his face.

"Take it easy, Lydia," I said. I felt like the stereotype of a brave brother patting his anguished sister on the shoulder. I felt foolish as hell, but death has a way of making almost anything seem foolish. "Sit down, honey," I said. "Here, sit down." I steered her over to an easy chair alongside the broken aquarium, snatching a cigarette from the canister on the coffee table and lighting it for her. She accepted it gratefully, sucking in a deep drag. There were no tears in her eyes, but she was still trembling.

The buzzer sounded.

"Yes?"

"I have the police on eight, sir."

"Thank you." I snapped off the toggle and picked up the phone, stabbing the button on the instrument with my fore-finger. "Hello."

"Sixteenth precinct, Sergeant Macgregor speaking."

"I'd like…" I hesitated. "Homicide, please."

"Just a moment, sir," the voice said.

I listened while a series of clicks filled the line, and then a smooth voice said, "Homicide, this is Sergeant Callighan."

"I want to report a murder," I said.

His voice was matter of fact. "Your name, sir?"

"Joshua Blake."

"Where are you now, sir?"

I gave him the address.

"Don't touch anything, sir," he said. "We'll send someone right over."

As simple as that. I put the phone back in its cradle, and we began waiting for the police.

Two uniformed cops arrived first. They were very polite about everything, coming into the office only after they'd stopped at the reception desk and asked for me. Once inside, they asked only if I was the one who'd made the call. When I told them I was, they took down my name, and then one went outside to post himself in the hallway, and the other took up a vigil near Del's body.

The detective arrived about five minutes later.

He was a tall, plain-looking man in a tweed suit. I won-dered why he wore tweeds in the middle of the summer, but I didn't bother asking him. He had straight blond hair that fell over one eye, and which he constantly pushed off his forehead with a long, tapering hand. His eyes were blue, set deep in his head, straddling his thin nose. He looked very much like a file clerk.

"I'm Detective-Sergeant Di Luca," he stated. "Did you make the call, sir?"

"Yes, I did."

"Who's this?" He gestured at Kennedy with a slight movement of his head.

"Tim Kennedy, my executive editor."

"And the young lady?" He glanced at her quickly, his eyes avoiding the obvious thrust of her breasts beneath the clinging linen jacket.

"My secretary."

"Would you mind sending them out, please?"

"Not at all. Tim, Lydia, would you…"

They moved toward the door silently, the way people will move in a funeral parlor or a museum.

When the door had closed after them, Di Luca asked, "Who's the dead man?"

"Del Gilbert, my partner."

Di Luca produced a small pad from his inside coat pocket. "Full name, please."

"Delano Gilbert."

"And your name, sir?"

"Joshua Blake."

He wrote it down and said, "Odd name. Joshua, I mean. New England?"

"Boston."

"Mmm. You found the body, Mr. Blake?"

"Yes, I did."

"When was this?"

"About twenty minutes ago."

"Touch anything?"

"No. Just the phone and the intercom. Nothing near…near the body."

Di Luca turned his head quickly, and his eyes shifted from Del's body to the broken aquarium, and then back to the body again.

"This the way you found it?" he asked the uniformed cop.

"Yes, sir."

He turned back to me. "Mr. Blake, what time did you…"

The buzzer sounded on Del's desk. I said, "Excuse me," and clicked the toggle.

"Mr. Lewis on seven," Jeanette said.

"Thank you." I picked up the phone and said, "Hello, Alex, how are you?"

"Got a few yarns here I like, Del," Alex said drily.

"Oh? Which ones?"

"Fellow name of Paley. Pretty good, you know, Del?"

I realized, then, that he thought he was talking to my partner. The realization sent a shiver up my spine, because my partner was lying on the rug, dead. "Alex," I said, "this is Josh."

"Oh, hello, Josh. You handle this fellow Paley?"

"I know his work."

"Got two here of his. One called *Death is My Maiden,* Know it?"

"Yes, yes, a good story." I glanced uneasily at Di Luca and shrugged.

"The other one is called *Shoot, Crap!* I'll have to change that title, Josh." Alex chuckled a little and then added quickly, "A hundred all right on each of these?"

"Yes, fine."

"O-kay," he said, breaking the word in two, "I'll put a check through."

"Thanks a lot, Alex."

I hung up, opening Del's desk drawer and writing the sales down on a pad. When I finished writing, I noticed that Di Luca was staring at me. "A few sales," I said. Then, in further explanation, I added, "We sell stories. That's our business."

"Oh? Must be interesting."

"Yes. Yes, it is."

"What time did you get in this morning, Mr. Blake?"

"Close to nine-thirty," I said.

"You usually come in about that time?"

"No, usually a little later. I'm expecting a big deal to close soon, and I wanted to be here to take any important calls."

"Did you come directly into this office?"

"No, I went into my own office next door."

"What brought you in here?"

"I wanted to check something in the safe."

"Did you expect your partner to be in so early?"

"No. I didn't expect him at all. I thought he was still out of town."

"Say," Di Luca said unexpectedly. "What part of Boston?"

"Huh?"

"You said you came from Boston. What part?"

"Oh. Not really from Boston. I come from a suburb. West Newton. Do you know it?"

"No. Where was your partner supposed to be?"

"In Connecticut. With a client."

"What did you want from the safe?" Di Luca asked.

"A contract. I wanted to check a contract to see when it expired."

"Did you check it?"

"No."

"What else do you keep in the safe?"

"Contracts, agreements, important documents. That's about all."

"Money?"

"No."

"What time did you get in this morning?" he asked.

"Nine-thirty." I stopped and looked at him curiously. "I already told you that."

Di Luca smiled and shook his head as if he were confused. "Yes, yes, so you did." He pulled a handkerchief from his back pocket and wiped it across his brow. "Hot as hell, isn't it?"

"Yes," I agreed.

"Paper says it's going to hit ninety-eight again. Man shouldn't have to work in this kind of weather."

"Well, if you don't…"

The buzzer sounded again, and I clicked on the intercom.

"Yes?"

"A Mr. Donato for Mr. Gilbert, sir."

"Who?"

"Mr. Donato, sir."

"I don't know him. Ask him what company he represents, will you?"

"Yes, sir."

I waited for several moments while Jeanette checked. Then her voice came over the intercom again. "Universal Photostats, sir."

"Univer…oh hell, I'll talk to him. What's he on?"

"Five, sir."

I picked up the phone and said, "Hello, this is Mr. Blake, Mr. Gilbert's partner. Can I help you?"

The man spoke with a faint Italian accent. "The photostats you ordered are ready," he said.

"What photostats?"

"Mr. Gilbert, he ordered…"

"Oh, okay. What's your address, I'll send a kid down for them."

He gave me the address, a number on East Forty-seventh

Street, and I told him I'd send one of our messengers over later. I wrote the number on a pad as I spoke, and when I hung up, Di Luca was watching me again.

"You'd better tell your girl not to disturb us," he said.

"What?"

"You'd better tell her not to…"

"I heard you. How the hell am I supposed to run a business if I can't take calls? I told you the reason I came in early was to…"

"What do you suppose your partner was doing here?"

"I don't know. Maybe he got in early this morning and came straight to the office."

"I doubt it," Di Luca said.

"Why?"

He gestured at the desk lamp with a limp wave of his hand. "Did you turn on that lamp when you came in this morning?"

"Why…" I turned and looked at the lamp, noticing for the first time that it was lighted.

"No. No, why should I do that?"

"No reason. I didn't think anyone would turn on a light in the morning, especially in a sunny office like this one. I figure maybe your partner came in during the night."

"Why would he do that?"

Di Luca shrugged. "What client?" he asked.

"Huh?"

"You said your partner was out of town. You said he was with a client."

"I said that? Yes, I guess I did."

"You did," Di Luca said, nodding. "Who was the client? Maybe that has something to do with his barging in here in the middle of the night."

"Cam Stewart. A Western writer."

"Cam Stewart, huh? Is that right?"

"You know Stewart?"

"I've read a few Draw Hudsons. Writes a good story."

"The editors seem to think so." For no good reason, that came out more sharply than I'd intended it. Di Luca lifted an eyebrow and smiled quizzically. Then he turned his back to me and walked over to where Del was stretched out before the couch.

"This is the way you found him, huh?"

"Just like that."

"With all this crap on the floor? With the safe open like this?"

"Yes."

"Mmm. Well, you can put that junk back in the safe, if you like." I started to do that, and Di Luca asked again. "This is the way you found it?"

"Just the way you see it."

"Looks like someone wanted something in that safe, doesn't it?"

"I don't see what," I said. "Just contracts in there. Certainly nothing of value to anyone but the agency."

"Nothing to kill a man for, huh?"

"Not that I can think of."

"How long you been partners?"

"Five years."

"What's the setup?"

"Usual partnership setup. Why?"

"Just curious."

"You can get your mind off that track," I snapped. "He's survived by a wife. I wouldn't gain a thing."

"I didn't say you would," Di Luca said mildly.

The buzzer sounded again, and he added, "Tell her no more calls this morning."

I walked to the desk and shoved down the toggle angrily.

"Sir, it's Mr. Sarran on six."

"Tell him nobody's in," Di Luca said into the intercom, leaning over the desk. "And any other calls you get, tell them you're all alone. No one's in yet. Have you got that?"

"Listen…" I started.

"This is a police officer," Di Luca said. "Do as I say."

He snapped off the toggle, and I glared at him. "What the hell was that for? I'm expecting some important calls."

"If they're that important, they'll call back."

"I thought you people were supposed to…"

"Was the fish tank busted when you came in?"

"Yes," I answered, a little sulkily.

"Who'd want to break a fish tank?"

"I'm sure I don't know."

Di Luca smiled. "I'm sure I don't know, either," he said.

He walked across the room, kneeling down to examine some of the still fish on the rug. "Shame," he said. "Some nice angel fish. And here's a neon tetra. Shame."

He stood up, walking around behind the tank. "Partner liked tropical fish, huh?"

"I never asked him. If a man keeps fish, I guess he likes them."

"What else did he keep?"

"I don't follow you."

"A dog, a cat? A mistress? Men keep lots of things."

I thought of Lydia, and a frown came onto my face. "Why do you ask?"

Di Luca walked across the room. "Somebody came in here and fired five shots at your partner. There has to be a reason for…"

"Five shots?" I'd only seen three, and they were all in Del's head.

"Two went through the fish tank," Di Luca said. "They're buried in the wall behind the tank. You know where the other three are."

"Oh," I said softly.

"So someone killed your partner. I'm trying to find a reason. You said there was nothing valuable in the safe. All right, I'll accept that for the time being. That means money wasn't a consideration. There are usually some pretty simple motives for murder, Mr. Blake. Money is one of them. There's jealousy, love, injured pride, rage, to mention a few of them."

"Love? Love is a murder motive?"

Di Luca smiled again. "You're a literary agent," he said, "You should know that 'each man kills the thing he loves.' "

"Yes. Yes, of course. That's just a literary allusion, though…"

"Money's out. For now, anyway. Maybe it'll be in again after we do a little more snooping around. We're great for snooping around. We can get real pesty. So it has to be another reason. There's always a motive. No one kills for the fun of it, except the psychopath. Of course, that's a consideration, too. But we look for motives first. When we're dealing with a psychopath, it gets a little harder."

"I thought all murderers were psychopaths," I said.

Di Luca reached into his jacket pocket, and pulled out a cigarette. He put it between his thin lips, lit it, and blew out a stream of smoke. "Hell, no," he said. "You could be a murderer as well as I. For all I know, you may be *the* murderer."

"And so might you."

"Sure, but it's pretty unlikely."

"Admittedly."

"To get back, what else did he keep?"

"Just fish," I said.

"How was his home life?"

"I don't know. We didn't mix business with pleasure."

"That's sensible."

"It worked best for us."

"Do you know his wife?"

"Yes."

"What's her name?"

"Gail. Gail Gilbert."

Di Luca cocked his head to one side. "That's very alliterative. Very pretty."

I didn't say anything. I walked across the room, peered behind the fish tank, and saw the holes the bullets had knocked out of the plaster.

"They're there, all right," Di Luca said. "What's she like?"

I was at the point where I could halfway follow his abrupt shifts in questioning. "She's a nice gal," I said.

"But?"

"But nothing."

"How well do you know her?"

"Fairly well."

"I thought you didn't mix socially?"

"We don't usually. A few parties now and then. To celebrate a big deal, most of the time."

I didn't tell him that Gail Gilbert was a restless woman, a woman who'd snap up another man eagerly, because of what Del was doing. But then, he hadn't asked.

"I guess you'd better go home, Mr. Blake," he said.

"What?"

"You'll only be underfoot here. Coroner will be here shortly, plus the photogs, and the boys dusting for prints—though I'm sure we won't find a hell of a lot. Not with that crowd you had in here fingering up the whole office. Never hurts, though. The boys like to dust. Makes them feel like private eyes."

"How'd you ever become a cop, Di Luca?"

He smiled. "How'd you ever become a literary agent?"

"I like stories."

Di Luca stopped smiling. "I like murder stories."

We stood a few feet apart, looking at each other. Then Di Luca walked to the door and opened it. "Go home, Mr. Blake. Go home and relax."

"And my business?"

"You have a phone at home?" He didn't wait for an answer. "Use that for your business. This is my business, and it's more important than yours at the moment."

"I guess that's an order, isn't it?"

He shrugged. "Send in your executive editor. I want to talk to him. And tell Lady Godiva to stick around. Few questions I want to ask her, too. In fact, ask everyone to stay until I've talked to them."

"Sure," I said.

"I'll give you a call, Mr. Blake. Leave your home number, won't you?"

"My secretary has it," I said. I closed the door behind me, and Lydia jumped off the couch and walked across the reception room quickly. Her eyes were wide, her breath coming hard. I watched her swivel toward me on her high heels, and I thought of Del, and wondered how many times he'd watched her swivel toward him, with or without heels.

"Josh," she said, "is…is…"

"Sherlock Holmes has everything under control," I said. "He wants to see all of you, one at a time. Tim first, then you. Pass the word, will you? And give Sherlock my home number."

"You're going home?"

"Yes."

"But…"

"Get Tim for him, will you?"

"But Josh…"

"Give me a call at home later. Let me know what Scotland Yard uncovers."

"You don't sound very goddamned heartbroken," she snapped. It came suddenly, and it hit me right between the eyes.

"I guess I'm not, very," I said.

"He was your partner," she threw at me.

"Gilbert didn't care much for Sullivan, either. Call me, Lydia. So long."

I walked out, rang for the elevator, and stood waiting for it, looking out the hallway window, over the rooftops of the city. The heat clung in a heavy miasma that smothered the steel and concrete. I thought of Del, and how lucky he was. He was cold.

I shook my head, pushing the elevator button again. Lydia's words had disturbed me. I really should have cared more. After all, he *had* been my partner. But somehow I couldn't quite muster up the sorrow necessary for such an occasion. Del Gilbert was an out-and-out bastard. He had screwed more writers than I could count on my fingers and toes, even though the agency's success was partly due to his tactics. He was also a lascivious rat who made a grab for every girl who went into his office. But Lydia had grabbed back, and Gail Gilbert was left holding the sag in her marriage. He had alienated more editors than there were magazines, and had somehow managed to get all those he'd feuded with fired on one pretext or another. Somehow, he'd hit on the remarkable idea that the chain of command was only as strong as the man who forged it. He'd brown-nosed every publisher in the business, and if an editor gave him trouble, he went straight to the publisher, and the editor was looking for a new job in ten minutes. That was the way he'd worked, and his methods got results.

A little of it had rubbed off on me, I guess. I'd changed a great deal since I first joined up with Del—but I hadn't changed completely. Which was another reason for the agency's phenomenal rise. Whereas editors were all so much dirt to Del, I treated them like human beings. Between us, we had them by the well-knowns. Those who liked me as a person brought their business to the agency. And those who feared Del's power also brought their business to the agency. No matter how you spelled it, they were bringing business to the agency.

That didn't change my mind about Del, though. I didn't like the hold he had on so many of the editors, and I'd told him about it more than once. He'd told me to quit if I wanted to— but he'd also reminded me of the clause in our partnership agreement. It was a simple one. The partnership could be dissolved at any time, but if it were not dissolved by mutual consent, then the dissolving partner forfeited the business name and agreed not to establish a competitive business for a period of six months after the dissolution.

I shoved my way into the elevator and took it down to the main floor.

Del was dead now, and Gail would probably want no part of the agency. She'd probably sell me her share for a flat sum and a percentage, and that was certainly all right with me.

I walked up to Eighth, cursing the heat, and cursing the stupid cop Di Luca with his goddamn tweed suit and his jumpy questioning. He was probably putting Tim through the same wringer by this time, and I wondered just what he hoped to accomplish by grilling everyone in the office. It occurred to me then that I was probably a prime suspect, and the idea amused me. Josh Blake, murderer.

I was still smiling when I piled into the Buick and drove oat of the garage with the top down. I was also sweating. It took me a good twenty minutes to get crosstown again, and by that time I was soaked to the skin. I took the East River Drive, heading uptown, thankful for the faint breeze that blew off the river, glad that the traffic was thin and I could keep the car moving at a fairly rapid clip.

I didn't notice the cab behind me until I'd turned off the Drive at Ninety-sixth Street, It caught my eye, and then I forgot it.

Until I made a left and saw it make a left, too.

For a moment, I thought Di Luca had sent some of his gum-shoes after me, but it seemed unlikely that cops would use a cab. As an experiment, I took a tight turn at the next corner.

The cab turned right, too.

That settled it. I cut crosstown, the heat beginning to close in on the car again. I turned right on Third Avenue, left again at the next corner, then left on Lexington. I drove downtown on Lex for three blocks, took a right to Madison, another right on Madison, and then back across to Second, after two blocks on Madison.

It didn't do any good. The cab was still behind me.

I began to get a little worried. The memory of Del's body was still fresh in my mind, and I expected the cab to pull up alongside at any moment, machine guns blasting, the way I'd seen it a dozen times in the movies. I was sweating freely, and I didn't know whether or not the heat was causing it. I kept an anxious eye on the rear-view mirror, waiting for the cab to pull up. It didn't. It kept a respectable distance behind me, and I began to realize I wasn't going to become a target.

Then why was I being followed?

I tried to take my mind off the cab. I thought of a nice cool drink at home, with the electric fan blowing on my bare legs as I sat in my shorts.

The cab didn't leave me.

I began to relax a little, and finally I said the hell with it.

The cabbie had glue on his grille, and I could lead him a chase all over the city, and we'd still wind up together in front of my apartment. I headed straight for it, with the cab in the rear view mirror all the way down to the building.

When I pulled into the garage under the house, I saw the cab slow down and then drive past, just as if the bastard hadn't been tailing me for the past half hour. I couldn't see who was in the back seat.

I cut the ignition, wiped the sweat from my forehead, and then started for the elevator and the drink awaiting me upstairs.

3.

I didn't expect to find Gail Gilbert there.

There was a drink, too, but it was firmly clutched in Gail's hand, her crimson fingertips curved around it. She shook the glass a little, and the ice clinked against the sides, and the brown liquid sloshed over the top, running down the sweating sides of the glass.

She was sitting, or I should say sprawling, in the chair near the bar. The doors on the bar were open, the fluorescent lights dancing on the clean, glistening rows of glasses inside. A bottle of brandy rested on top of the bar, with its cork upturned next to it. Alongside the bar, the doors on the television-radio-phonograph console were wide open, as if she'd gone to that by error, mistaking it for the bar unit which was its twin.

Gail Gilbert is an attractive woman. She looked particularly appealing this morning. She wore her hair cut close to her head, carefully clipped to give a careless, casual, wind-blown appearance. This morning it looked more tousled than ever, either by accident or design. It curled close to her neck, spilled onto the whiteness of her forehead, framed the oval of her face like a churning black sea embracing a small white sailboat.

She was wearing a pale blue denim duster, and I wondered if every woman in the city of New York had suddenly lost her marbles. First the girl earlier this morning, wearing nylon stockings when the thermometer mercury was ready to over-flow, and now Gail wearing a duster fastened tight around her with three buttons: one at the throat, another smack between her full breasts, and the third just about where her navel should be. Her head was thrown back against the cushions, with her cameo nose pointed at the ceiling, her lips parted slightly over even, white teeth. Her eyes were closed when I came in, and she didn't stir as I crossed the room. Her legs were stretched out in front of her, long, curving, accentuated by the dark blue heels she wore. The duster was tucked down between her legs, outlining the fluid curve of her thighs.

"Good morning," I said.

She lifted her head slowly, stared across the room at me, tilting one raven eyebrow onto the smooth curve of her brow.

"Hello, hello," she said, her voice slurred. I realized then that she was carrying a snootful, and I began to wonder just what the hell she was doing here. I also wondered if she knew someone had thoughtlessly let the blood out of Del's head. I took off my jacket and tossed it over to the couch. My shirt was soaked through to the skin, and I unbuttoned it, pulling it out of my trousers. I tossed my tie onto the jacket, and then took off the shirt.

"Hope you don't mind, Gail," I said, not really giving a damn whether she did or not. "This heat. How can you stand a coat in the house?"

"Not a coat," she said, smiling. "S'duster."

I walked to the bar, filled a tall glass with ice, and then spilled brandy over it. I took a long swig before I spoke again.

"How'd you get in?"

"Key," she said.

"Key?"

"You gave one to Del a long time ago. 'Member when he had to pick up some stuff here?"

I vaguely remembered an office emergency, when I had to hold the fort, and I'd given Del a key to my place. "Mmm, I remember."

"Little Gail remembered, too."

"How long have you been here?"

"Not long enough," she said. "Got here too late. I wanted to catch you before you left."

"Oh? Why? What's up?"

She swirled the drink in her glass again, and the ice made little tinkling sounds. It was stifling in the room, even though she'd had the fan on. Its tiny electric hum filled the air now, hung between us like an Oriental chant. I could feel the perspiration pouring down my bare chest. I took another swig of the brandy, enjoying the cold feel of the ice against my lips.

"Sauce for the goose," she said. She leaned forward, putting her drink down on the arm of the chair, then gripping both arms of it to pull herself up. She had a little difficulty. She stretched out her legs, and the duster pulled back over her knees, showing the curving fullness of both calves. No stockings. Gail was a sensible girl. She finally got to her feet, wobbled unsteadily for a moment, and made her way to the coffee table. She leaned over to remove a cigarette from the container there, and her breasts pushed out against the denim of the duster.

"How do you mean?" I asked. I really wasn't listening to what she said. I was thinking *She knows about Del, and she's trying to drown it with brandy.* I was also thinking I wanted to call the office to make sure any important calls would get routed to my home number.

"Del," she said, putting the cigarette between her lips.

"Yes," I said. "Hell of a thing." I should have said more, I know, but I'm never good at giving condolences.

"One hell of a thing," she agreed. She looked down at the coffee table, her glance running right over the lighter alongside the cigarette box. "Say, can't a girl get a goddamn light?" she asked.

I reached over, handing her the lighter. "Help yourself, Gail," I said. "I want to make a call."

Gail, clicking away at the lighter while I dialed, succeeded in getting a few feeble sparks but no flame. I was waiting for Jeanette to answer when Gail walked over to me, handing me the lighter.

"Do this for me, will you?"

I took the lighter, thumbed it into flame. Gail put one arm on the chair behind me, leaned over. She pressed her knee against my thigh, and I looked up into her face, a little puzzled. Her eyes were closed as she drew in on the cigarette. For a moment, I thought I'd mistaken the pressure of her knee. Then Jeanette's voice came onto the line.

"Gilbert and Blake, good morning."

"This is Mr. Blake," I said. "Are the police still there?"

"Yes, sir."

"Are they finished with Tim?"

"Yes."

"And Lydia?"

"She just left for home, sir."

"All right, Jeanette. Listen, if there are any calls, will you give them my home number and ask them to call here? I'll be here most of the day."

"Yes, sir."

"Have there been many calls?"

"Several, sir."

"Want to read them off?"

I waited while Jeanette got the list of calls. Gail stood close to me, her brow lined with confusion. "Did you say police?" she asked.

"Yes," I said. "They've been all over the goddamned office, like rats climbing out of the wood…"

"I've got those calls, sir," Jeanette interrupted.

"Let's have them."

"Mr. Sarran called."

"Sarran? Who the hell is Sarran?"

"R. J. Sarran, the book critic, he said."

"Who else called?"

"Mr. Donato, about the photostats again."

"Who else?"

"James Finch at Harper and Brothers."

"What did he want?"

"He didn't say."

"He can wait. Who else?"

"A woman at Street and Smith. About a release for some science-fiction anthology."

"Anyone else?"

"No, sir."

"Dave Becker, Carlyle Rutherford, Cam Stewart?"

"No, sir, none of them."

"If any of the three call, give them my home number. If anyone else calls, just tell them Mr. Gilbert has had an accident and the office will be closed today. Got that?"

"Yes, sir, Mr. Becker, Mr. Rutherford, and Mr. Stewart. I have that, sir."

"Good girl. 'Bye, Jeanette."

I didn't wait for an answer. I cradled the phone and turned to Gail. I found her with her eyes wide and her mouth open.

"Wh…what did you just say?"

"About what?"

"About…Del. About…about an accident."

It hit me like a falling boulder. Good Christ, she hadn't known Del was dead. And I'd broken it to her in the worst possible way. In fact, I'd done worse than simply break it to her, clean and crisp. I'd hinted at it on the phone, and now the worst part was still ahead of me.

"Gail…" I bit down on my lip, crossed the room and killed the brandy left in my glass. The ice had already melted down, leaving the drink flat and weak.

"What is it?" she asked. She was holding her glass tightly, and her knuckles were white, the skin pulled taut against the bone.

"Del's dead," I said quickly.

It was almost as if I'd hit her in the stomach. She backed away from me a few paces, still holding to the glass the way she'd hold to a life preserver. She closed her eyes tightly, leaned against the bar, and bent her head. She didn't say anything for a long while.

Then, as if she'd finally gripped her insides together, she looked up and asked, "How?"

"Three bullets in his head. I found him this morning when I…"

"Who?"

"I don't know. The police are on it now."

I expected her to cry, or scream, or something. She just stood there, though, and said, "It takes a while to get used to it."

"Yeah."

"Especially when I came here to…to…"

She stopped speaking, turned rapidly and filled her glass again.

"You'd better go easy," I said.

She tossed off the brandy in one gulp, then turned to fill her glass once more.

"Gail…"

"Shut up, Josh. Please shut up. Just let me do what I want to do, and shut up. Please, Josh."

She took another fast swallow, and then began nursing the

drink, sipping at it slowly, rolling the glass between her hands. There was sweat on her brow, and the duster clung to the lines of her body, hung there limply.

I could hear the buzz of the fan, insistent, like flies attacking a felled horse. The ticking of my watch was loud in the room. The heat seemed to magnify everything, throwing it back into the face like a petroleum explosion.

She didn't look at me. She stared at an invisible spot in the rug, rolling the glass, clinking the ice.

"I'm glad," she said at length.

"What?"

"I'm glad. I'm glad someone killed the bastard."

There was a moment of silence in the room, and then the shrill clamor of the telephone sliced into the air, shredding the silence, leaving nothing but the heat.

I lifted the receiver. "Yes?"

"Mr. Blake?"

"Yes."

"Di Luca."

"Who?"

"Di Luca. You know. Sherlock Holmes."

"Oh."

"We're just about finished here, Mr. Blake. We'll be carting the body away in a few minutes, and I'll be leaving some of the boys to give the place a thorough going-over. Thought you'd like to know."

"Thanks," I said.

"Who was the guy you threw out?"

"What? I'm sorry, I…"

"This morning. Some guy was up with a book. You tossed him out on his can. What was his name?"

"Oh, him. I don't remember."

"Mr. Blake, we can…"

"Gunnison," I said, remembering abruptly. "That was his name. Why?"

"No special reason. He was sore, huh?"

"He was sore, and I was sorer."

"Got a bad temper, Mr. Blake?"

"Only when I'm being pestered," I snapped.

Di Luca chuckled. "Your partner ever pester you?" he asked.

"Look, Mr. Law," I said, "are you insinuating…"

"Nothing of the sort. I never insinuate, Mr. Blake. I book or I don't book. But I never hint."

"Are you booking me?"

"Not yet."

"Then I'm busy."

"Mmm," he said. "Me too. Goodbye, Mr. Blake."

I slammed the phone down and said, "That goddamned petty tyrant. The police force is full of…"

"They don't know yet?" Gail asked.

"They've got a Cro-Magnon in charge of the investigation," I said, pouring more brandy. "With him around, they'll never know."

"Did you hear what I said before?"

"Yes," I said. "I heard."

"Well?"

"You're looped. You don't know what the hell you're talking about."

"I'm not looped. I wasn't looped when I first got here, either. I *was,* after waiting for you—but not when I got here, and not now. I could drink a vat of 69 and not be looped."

"Well, that's fine. If you're not looped, you're insane."

"Come off it, Josh."

"I don't follow you, Gail."

"Del was a bastard," she said. "I'm glad someone shot him. I'd have done it myself, eventually. Someone just saved me the trouble."

"You'd better not tell that to Sherlock."

"Who?"

"Mr. Di Luca. The Inspector-General. Sam Spade, Phil Marlowe, and Perry Mason all rolled into one."

"Why not tell him? It's what I think. I'll tell anyone what I think," Gail said. She swallowed another big gulp of brandy, winced as it went down. "God, I wish I could get drunk again. Goddamn it, you've taken the edge off my high."

"You'd better go home," I said. "Di Luca should be looking you up pretty soon. He'll suspect we got together to plan Del's murder if he finds you here. His moronic mind works that way."

"We didn't, though, did we?"

"What the hell are you talking about?"

"Nothing. Forget it. Do you know why I came here?"

"No."

"I suddenly got fed up, Josh. Right up to here." She passed one slender hand across her throat, "I said to myself, 'If Del can roll in the hay with that auburn bitch, then I can...' "

"Cut it out, Gail."

"Why? You know it's true, and I know it. That's the worst part. If I hadn't known, I'd have been better off."

"Gail!"

"She's as much to blame as he is," Gail snapped. "Del was a chippie chaser, but Lydia..."

"For Christ's sake, Gail..."

"Oh, I know she wasn't the only one, Josh. But she was the big one, the *grand amour*, the ready, steady slut."

"Gail, he's dead. There's nothing more, nothing to..."

"I know. I know, and I'm glad. Friday night I figured it all out. He told me he was going to see another client, but I knew damn well it was a woman again. Not Lydia this time." She chuckled again. "I wonder if auburn Lydia knew."

"He *was* with a client," I said.

"No, Josh. A woman. I know."

"Look, Gail, give the devil his due. Del was with a client. He went up to see one of our Western writers. *I know*."

"I say a woman, but I won't argue. I don't need excuses, anyway. If he wasn't with a woman these past few days, it's the first time he wasn't. I decided two could play the game. It took me a long time to decide. I tossed on an empty bed all weekend long. And then I decided, and here I am."

"Why?" I asked.

Gail Gilbert smiled, and there was the age-old look in her eyes, the look that had given Samson a haircut and Rhett a severe pain in the Civil War. She didn't say anything, but it was all there in the slope of her eyes, in the careless tilt of her hips, in the tongue-moist wetness of her lips.

Her hands moved rapidly to the buttons on her duster.

"Look, Josh," she said.

The duster fell away from her breasts, parting like curtains, showing the Gail Gilbert that only Del had known thus far. The denim clung to the globes of her breasts for a brief instant. She brushed the duster aside with an angry movement, and it swirled back over her hips, revealing a flat, hard stomach, a shadow-filled navel, firm, crimson-tipped breasts high on her chest.

"This is why I came."

Her voice was low, and the muscles on her stomach shivered. She took a step closer to me, and it could have been a hell of a dramatic moment if the phone hadn't decided to shrill again.

I picked up the receiver quickly, unsure of my emotions, watching as Gail walked closer to me.

"Hello?"

"Blake?"

"Yes."

"This is Carlyle Rutherford. What the hell is going on at your office?"

"A little trouble," I said vaguely. Rutherford was the Hollywood agent who was handling the movie rights to the Cam Stewart property. He, of course, stood to lose a goodly commission if the deal fell flat. "You're not calling from the Coast, are you?"

"I just got into the city. What's this latest nonsense of yours?"

"What nonsense?"

Gail stopped about three inches from my chair, and dropped the duster to the floor. It fell in a blue heap at her feet, and she looked like an alabaster statue in a small garden pool.

"It's still sauce for the goose," she whispered. "Dead or not."

"Who's there with you?" Rutherford asked.

"No one," I said. At the same moment, Gail stepped behind my chair and put her arms around my neck. I felt her warm skin against my bare back, and then her, lips trailed across my neck, her breath standing my hair on end.

"What's this new business about twenty-five percent, Blake?"

I tried to move away from Gail, but she had me in a hammer lock, and her tongue was playing with my ear now, and her hands were roving over my chest, smoothly, easily. "Just what it sounds like, Rutherford. We want twenty-five percent of the movie deal."

"You must be out of your mind."

"I'd hardly say that, Rutherford." I stood up abruptly, lifting the phone and moving away from Gail. "We control the TV rights to those books, and we intend to use them."

"This is highway robbery, Blake."

"Maybe so. If you want a release of the TV rights, though, you'll have to do it our way."

Gail was back again. Only this time, she wasn't behind me. She stood in front of me, her breasts pressing against my chest. She placed her hands on my hips, and she pulled herself toward me and buried her lips in the side of my neck.

"Hang up," she whispered.

I wanted to shove her away, but I was also half tempted to hang up. Her body was warm, but it made me forget the heat that was everywhere around us.

"Well, get this, Blake," Rutherford said. "I'm not going to put up with any of your damned shenanigans. Your practices are pretty well known throughout the field, and I'll be damned if you're going to get away with another hijack."

"Hang up," Gail whispered urgently.

"I'd be careful what I say," I warned Rutherford.

"I'll say whatever the hell I damn please to a crook like you."

I could feel Gail's breath on my face, warm, ragged. She kissed my cheek, and I listened to Rutherford's drone, and I wondered which was the reality. Gail Gilbert in my arms. Gail Gilbert, my partner's wife. My dead partner's wife. Warm, and alive, and wanting. Or Rutherford, going on and on and on.

"…the deal goes through exactly as we first planned it, and if you don't care for the terms, you can just stuff it."

"Uh-uh, Rutherford. You're forgetting one little thing."

"What's that, Blake?"

"A little item that puts the deal in my lap, and not yours. If you…"

Gail's hands were warm, and her lips were insistent. She planted quick kisses along the line of my jaw, allowed her lips to trail over my chin, ducking her head beneath the telephone receiver as I moved it out of her way unconsciously.

"What was that?" Rutherford asked.

"Just this," I said. "I want Dave Becker to make the pilot film for television, and he'll agree to that or he'll never get to make a Draw Hudson movie."

"Draw Hudson…" Rutherford started.

"Draw Hudson is the hottest Western character today. He's in every one of Cam Stewart's books, and I control the TV rights to those books. If Becker won't agree to my terms, I'll sell Hudson to the highest bidder, and you know what that'll mean."

"Blake, you can't…"

"I damn well can, and I will. Your potential audience will see Hudson on its TV set once every week, and the TV people will be free to choose incidents from any one of the books. That'll leave your producer Becker with a movie property worth exactly beans. For Christ's sake, Gail!"

"What, Blake?"

"Nothing." I elbowed Gail away, and she came back at me with sleepy eyes, long lashes touching, lips parted and moist. "I'm being generous as it is, Rutherford. I've agreed to pay for half the cost of the pilot film, but I don't like being left in the cold on the movie end. After all, this is valuable property, and there are two sides to the coin."

"Like what?"

"Like the possibility of the movies ruining the television sale of the property. If that happens, I'm left with a pilot film and an empty bag. Uh-uh—I want protection whichever way this deal works out."

"By that, you mean you want twenty-five percent of all the film profits."

"You hit it, Rutherford."

"And if we don't give you that?"

"You'll be up to your ears in lawsuits from the second you sign a contract."

"On what charge?"

"Infringement. I own the TV rights."

"Suppose we sign a contract excluding TV rights?"

"Don't be ridiculous, Becker wouldn't come near a contract like that."

"Maybe he would."

"You'll be laughed right out of the business. Go ahead, ask Becker if he'll sign for just movie rights. Make sure you tell him Draw Hudson will then go to the highest bidder. Ask him what he thinks."

"Well…"

"I've got you where it hurts, Rutherford. If you close the deal without me, I sue the pants off you. And you can't close without TV rights because no one is that foolish. You *have* to do business with me."

"You're referring to that agreement again, aren't you?"

"Correct, my friend. Signed by Cam Stewart."

"How do I know such an agreement exists? I've never even seen the goddamned thing!"

"You can take my word for it, Rutherford."

"In this business, Blake, I take no one's word. Least of all yours."

"Then drop by the office and I'll show it to you. We've got two copies of the thing. The original is in our office safe and…"

Gail chose that moment to push the phone away from my mouth and clamp her lips onto mine. It was something. It was really something. I forgot all about Del, and damn near all about Rutherford. I wrapped my loose arm around her, pulling her closer. Her lips were sweet and wet and expert and full of longing. I lost myself in her kiss, swallowed in a widening whirlpool that tried to pry my fingers loose from the phone receiver. Her breasts were riveted to my chest and her body moved frantically.

"Blake?" Rutherford's voice called from a long way off. "Blake?"

I lifted the receiver limply, pulled my lips reluctantly from Gail's. Gail could wait. Gail had been waiting a long time now.

"Yeah, Rutherford. I said I've got the original in the office safe and…"

Gail didn't interrupt me this time. An idea did. An idea and a picture. The picture was of Del Gilbert lying like a limp sack on the floor of his office, with the safe door wide and a sheaf of papers scattered all over the rug.

The safe. *Open.*

"Well, Blake? Say, just what the hell is going on there?"

"I've got the agreement," I said, gulping hard. "One in the safe, and a photostat."

"I'll believe it when I see it," Rutherford said sharply. "You can reach me at the Astor, Blake. Goodbye."

He hung up, and his voice left my ear to be replaced by Gail's.

"At last," she murmured.

4.

I kept my hand on the cradled receiver, and Gail covered it with her own. She lifted her face, and her lips shone wetly. The heat had put a high sheen on her body, and it glistened now as the slanting rays of the sun streamed through the blinds.

"You'd better go home," I said.

She threw her arms around my neck, thrust her hips at me. "Uh-uh."

I disengaged her arms and pushed her gently away from me. "Gail," I said, "go home."

She stuck out her lower lip like a hurt child, and ducked her head. "I won't, Josh. It's taken me a long time to work up the courage for this. I'd have enjoyed it more if Del were alive, but I'm not going to stop because he's dead."

"Stop talking like a damn fool," I told her. "In the first place, you've got to be a Zulu to enjoy a bed in this weather, and in the second place, the police are going to be crawling all over your apartment in about zero minutes flat. It'll look real cozy if they find you here."

"The hell with the police."

"Sure. And the hell with the law, and the hell with murder, and…" I cut myself short and snapped my fingers, sidestepping Gail and heading for my locked desk. She followed me across the room, the sun playing subtle tricks with her hips. She seemed completely unaware of her nudity.

I fished in my trouser pocket for my key ring and said, "Where'd you dump your clothes, Gail? You'd better put something on."

"I came in the duster," she said defiantly.

That straightened me up, and I stared at her in disbelief. "Just the duster? Holy Jesus!"

"I told you why I came, Josh. I wasn't kidding. I'm still not kidding."

"Some other time, Gail. For God's sake, your husband was just murdered!"

"*Requiescat...*" she started.

"Look, Gail," I said, "you're a lovable wench. There's nothing I'd like to do better than you-know-what. Come back after Del is buried, and when the temperature has dropped to 150. Right now, unless you want to be up to your pretty nose in a murder rap, you'd better get the hell home."

She stared at me in silence for a few moments, and her eyes turned cold and forbidding. She seemed suddenly aware of her body, and she crossed her arms ineffectually over her breasts, the nipples peering at me like curious, snub-nosed children.

"Sure," she said. "If that's the way you want it."

"That's the way I want it."

She turned quickly, walked across the room with her head high. My eyes followed the sway of her buttocks in spite of myself, and I finally turned away and stuck a key into the desk lock. Behind me, I heard Gail rustling into the duster. I twisted the key and the flap of the desk dropped. I found a smaller key on the ring, inserted it into one of the cubbyhole drawers at the back of the desk. My fingers found the paper I wanted, and I removed it from the drawer quickly, unfolded it, and turned to let the sun hit it.

Gail was buttoning the duster, her back to me.

I looked at the paper. It was the photostat, all right, and it still gave the Gilbert and Blake Agency the sole and exclusive right to handle radio and TV rights to all the Cam Stewart books. That was good enough for me. I folded the stat in half, and then in half again.

"I'm leaving," she said

"I'll call you, Gail. I'll call you a little later."

She walked to the door, opened it quickly, and said, "Don't bother." The door slammed behind her, and I listened to her heels clicking along the outside corridor, to stop finally by the elevator bank. I took out my wallet and stuffed the stat into the zipper compartment, putting the wallet back into my pocket and buttoning the flap over the pocket. I walked into the bedroom, then took a clean shirt from the dresser drawer, and slipped into it. I took my tie from where I'd dropped it in the living room, knotted it hastily, and pulled on my jacket. I took a last look around the apartment and then left, locking the door behind me.

When I reached the elevator banks, Gail was gone.

A uniformed cop leaned against the entrance door to my office. His blue shirt was stuck to his chest, great circles of sweat starting under his armpits and merging over his breastbone. He looked tired, and hot, and sick of a silly job like watching an office *after* a man had been killed in it. I approached him warily. My previous experience with cops had come from three sources, namely: a) the stories our fertile writers concocted and which I then sold for fabulous and not-so-fabulous prices to the publishing field at large. The cops in these stories bore little or no resemblance to any police officer, living or dead. b) a ticket I'd received for speeding on the George Washington Bridge during World War II. I was in uniform and hurrying to get back to camp before I got on some sergeant's slop list. That didn't faze the cop a bit. He wrote out the ticket in his leisurely way, as if I wasn't already in the pit with the pendulum descending lower and lower. This cop also bore no resemblance to any police officer, living or dead. And c) Di Luca, the amiable hashish smoker from Scotland Yard in Manhattan.

This was not an auspicious background upon which to build a familiarity with the City's finest.

"Hello," I said.

The cop tilted his hat back on his head, and stared at me as if I were a praying mantis. I got the distinct impression that he'd have stepped on me if it weren't against the law. He had straight red hair, and the hair was matted against his forehead. He removed his cap, shoved the soggy red mass back onto the top of his skull where it belonged, and then put his hat on again. His eyes told me he was blaming *me* for his having worn his winter headgear on a sweltering summer day. "The office is closed," he said.

"I know."

"Then shove off."

"It's my office," I said.

"It's still closed. Mister, it's too damned hot to argue."

"Officer," I said, "there's something I'd like to check inside."

"And what was that?"

"Some papers in the safe."

"Well, forget them. If they're in the safe, they're safe. Besides, there's nobody in there but the police." He paused and eyed me accusingly. "And they're scrupulously honest."

"Without doubt," I said. "Only what I hope is in the safe may not be in the safe at all. In which case, the police might want to know about it."

"What's your name?" he asked.

"Blake. Joshua Blake."

He turned and looked at the lettering on the door. "Gilbert and Blake." He lifted his hat again, scratching his head with the fingers of the same hand. "Guess it was Gilbert who got it, huh?"

"Yes, I guess so."

"And you want to check something in the safe?"

"Yes."

He stared at me again. "I'll check inside," he said at last. He turned to open the door, muttering, "Jesus, what a beat!"

I lit a cigarette and waited outside for him. I'd taken about five drags on it when he appeared again. "All right," he said, "go on in. Don't touch nothing."

"Thanks," I said.

He was still muttering about his beat when I opened the door and walked into our reception room. It was strangely quiet. This was an eerie silence—the silence of a cathedral, the silence of a funeral parlor.

I walked through the long room quickly, opening the door to Del's office.

The sun knifed through the Venetians, laying long golden bars on the top of Del's desk. Behind the long desk sat Detective-Sergeant Di Luca, his hands clasped before him, his head bent to study the spot on the rug where Del had lain a few hours before.

He lifted his head when I came in, but he didn't say anything.

I closed the door gently behind me. "I didn't expect to find you here," I said.

Di Luca smiled wanly. "Nice and quiet here. Good for thinking."

I stifled a crack about the thinking ability of sub-species, and said instead, "I just remembered something. Mind if I look into the safe?"

"Not at all. The boys just left. Got a lot of nice fingerprints. Mostly your partner's. The rest are yours, I imagine, and your staff's."

"Staff all gone home?"

"Yes. You'd better keep the shop closed today. Better that way. What is it?"

"Huh?"

"The thing you remembered? In the safe."

"Oh. An agreement. I wondered if it was still…well, this may sound silly, but it was an important agreement, and…"

"And you think your partner was killed for it?"

"Well…"

"Well, the thought crossed your mind. Probably not a valid one, either. Most murder motives are fairly simple. The only complicated, carefully planned murders appear in detective fiction. I know. I read it."

"I read a little of it myself," I said sarcastically.

"I know. I've been looking through the bookcases in your office. Did you sell all of those books?"

"Yes."

Di Luca nodded appreciatively. I went to the wall safe to the left of the door leading to my office, quickly twirled the dial.

"You think someone forced him to open the safe, took what they wanted, and then shot him, is that it?"

"Something like that." I missed a number listening to him, and had to start all over again.

"Possible," Di Luca said. "That wouldn't explain all the wild shooting, though, would it?"

"Wild shooting?"

"Two shots in the fish tank. Doesn't necessarily depict a cool customer, does it?"

"Cool customers can have bad eyes," I said.

"Yes, yes." Di Luca pinched his nose with his thumb and forefinger. "Your partner was shot from the door, you know."

"I didn't know."

"Yes. Very scientific these days. We can figure exactly where a bullet came from, just what its trajectory was, all sorts of fancy things like that. Oh, we're busy little bees." He chuckled, and I twirled the dial to the right. "Do you own a Colt .45, Mr. Blake?"

"No," I said quickly.

"That's what killed your partner. Just asking."

I opened the safe and reached into the back for a pile of folders, neatly stacked beside a leather briefcase. I thumbed through the folders and selected one marked "Important Papers."

"Shot from the door," Di Luca said. "Implies that whoever did it simply popped in, blasted off, and then beat it."

"Whoever did it could also have been waiting by the door while Del went through the safe. Maybe the murderer stood by the door so that he could hear anyone who approached."

"You know a lot about it," Di Luca said.

I looked up wearily. "You're a crafty guy," I said. My voice was dull.

Di Luca shrugged. "Your important agreement there?"

I thumbed through the papers rapidly. "No," I said. Somehow, the discovery didn't excite me as much as I thought it would, and I attributed that to Di Luca's presence.

"Doesn't mean anything, of course," he said. "If it was that important, your partner may have taken it with him."

"I doubt it."

Di Luca shrugged again. "You see, it would have been impossible for Gilbert to be standing near the safe when he got it. If he had been, he'd have just fallen against the wall and slid down to the floor that way. We'd have found him on his knees. But your partner was stretched out in front of that couch. My guess is that he was sitting there when the killer came in. He got up when he saw the killer, was shot, and dropped in his tracks. Flat on his face."

"You didn't look very carefully," I said.

"Whuh?" Di Luca glanced at me casually.

"Your tricks are getting about as subtle as rivets, Di Luca, Del Gilbert was *lying on his back* when I found him."

"Oh? Is that right?"

"It's right, and you know damn well it's right."

Di Luca nodded. "Yes, I guess it is. Then he could have been at the safe, couldn't he? The bullets could have hit him and knocked him backward. That's possible, isn't it?"

"You're the cop," I said. "What about this missing paper?"

"I don't know," he said seriously. "What was it about?"

"An exclusive agreement giving us TV and radio rights to the Cam Stewart books."

"Do people in this business usually commit murder for signed papers?" he asked.

"How the hell should I know?"

He spread his hands wide. "And how the hell should I know? I'll have to think about it. The damned thing's probably misplaced, anyway. Why don't you go home, Blake?"

"I was just about to ask you the same thing."

"See? Our minds run along the same channels. Go on. I'll take care of your office for you."

"Well thanks. Thanks a million."

"I get paid for this," Di Luca said. "I never had it so good."

I rammed the folder back into the safe after taking another careful look through it. The agreement was gone, definitely. I closed the safe, twirled the dial, and turned to Di Luca.

"Don't forget to lock up," I said.

He nodded.

When I left the room, he was staring at the rug again, and the sun made a torch of his blond hair.

I said goodbye to the cop in the hall. He grunted and wiped his perspiring brow. I walked to the elevators, got into the first car that stopped, and headed for Lydia Rafney's place.

✿

Lydia lived in a swank apartment on the East River, an apartment that wasn't paid for by her salary. I know, because I made out the payroll every two weeks.

I was greeted at the door by a doorman who looked like a general in the German Army. He clicked his heels, completing the simile for me beautifully, opened the big glass doors, and waved one braided and scarlet uniform sleeve toward the switchboard in the lobby. I didn't know whether to tip him or salute him, so I simply walked in. I told the switchboard operator who I wanted to see, and he buzzed Lydia's apartment, cleared me, and ushered me toward the elevator banks.

A subordinate, something like a colonel, ran the elevator up to the tenth floor. He clicked his heels when he let me out, and I began to wonder if the janitor was in the basement peeling spuds. I found Lydia's door, pushed an ivory panel set in the jamb, and listened to four chimes sound within the apartment. While I waited, I thought about how cool it was here in the hallway, and I suddenly realized the place was probably air-conditioned. I jammed an impatient thumb at the panel again, listened to the same four bored, indifferent chimes.

There was a click in the center of the door, and I knew the lid of a peephole was being drawn back. I couldn't see any eye because it was one of those mirrored jobs, one-way glass that could be seen through only from the inside. There was another click as the lid fell home again, and then I heard the bolt snap and the door opened wide.

"Hello, Josh," Lydia said. Her voice was toneless, as if the heat had succeeded in wilting it. It was the only wilted thing about her, though. Her auburn hair was pulled back over her ears, piled onto the top of her head like strawberries on a white layer cake. Her face looked fresh-scrubbed, with her eyes a deep green above the sharp angles of her cheekbones. Lydia

owned a face that belonged in the women's magazines, mod-
eling expensive earrings or saucy hats. In the beginning, I used
to wonder why she wasted her time in a stuffy literary agency.
That was before I tipped to the little romance she and Del were
sharing.

"May I come in?" I asked.

"Certainly," she said.

She stepped back a few paces, and I followed her inside. She
looked set for an afternoon at the beach. She wore a strapless
halter that valiantly failed to cover the swell of her breasts,
hugging her like a boa constrictor. The halter was green, ac-
centing the color of her eyes, highlighting the dull flame of her
hair. She wore cuffed, white cotton shorts, just short enough to
emphasize the splendid curve of her slim legs. She turned and
walked into a drop living room, her leather sandals padding
over the thick rug on the floor.

"Drink, Josh?" she asked, not turning. She walked directly to
a marble-topped coffee table that screamed "Made in Italy,"
reached for the bottle there without waiting for my answer.

"A nice place you have," I said.

She kept her back to me, leaning over to pour, and my eyes
unconsciously followed the curve from thigh to neck. "That's
right," she said, "this is the first time you've been here."

She took ice from a bucket on the table, dropped it into the
glass, and then turned, extending the drink to me.

"Thanks," I said. I took a swallow of the whiskey. It was as
expensive as the rest of the apartment. She took her time pouring
herself a drink and then walked over to the grand piano in the far
corner of the room, leaning against it like a nightclub chanteuse
ready to go into her routine.

"So?" she asked.

"So, it's one hell of a thing."

"Yes."

"I guess I was a little callous at the office."

"That's all right."

"I mean, Del and I…"

"I said it was all right. Leave it at that." She reached behind her, slid the lid from a cigarette box, and removed an ivory-tipped cigarette which she placed between her lips. I moved toward the lighter on the coffee table, but she grabbed the one on the piano first and lit the cigarette herself. "Did you come to offer condolences, Josh?"

"No."

"Good thing. I'll survive, you know."

"I figured as much, Lydia."

"Funny how a thing like this pulls people together, isn't it? In the office, you hardly ever said two words to me. Now it's old home week, and everyone has gotten together for the big game. Think we'll win, Josh?"

"What do you mean?"

"I mean, think you'll get away with it?"

I didn't answer for a few seconds. Then, all I could manage was, "What!"

"Killing Del."

I shook my head. "I know *what* you meant, Lydia. I'd like to know what you meant *by* it, though."

"That's the logical reaction, I suppose. I didn't expect you to give a confession."

"You're being a little bit ridiculous. Maybe it's the heat."

"Sure, it's the heat. Tell me, Josh, what happens when one member of a partnership dies?"

"The partnership usually dissolves. Why?"

"And then what?"

"If there's a will, the estate usually gets…"

"And after that?"

"I don't follow."

"The surviving partner. What does he do?"

"Me, you mean?"

"In this case, yes. You."

"You tell me, Lydia. You're driving at *something*, aren't you?"

"The surviving partner might start his own agency. No partner this time. The surviving partner may figure that his share of a big movie deal will give him the extra lift he'd need. Mightn't he?"

"He might. But he didn't."

"There's only the surviving partner's word for that."

"And the murderer's."

"And they might be one and the same, mightn't they?"

"But they aren't."

"Again, we have only the…"

"Let's can it, Lydia," I said. "I didn't come here for this sort of crap."

"Why *did* you come?"

I reached into my pocket and pulled out my wallet. I took out the folded stat and handed it to Lydia.

"You remember this, don't you?"

She put her cigarette in an ashtray, blew out a stream of smoke, and then took the stat from my hand. She unfolded it, looked at it briefly, and nodded her head. "Yes. What about it?"

"Do you recall seeing the original?"

"Yes. It was in the safe."

"Did Del take it with him when he went to see Stewart?"

"Why?"

"I want to know."

"How should I know?"

"Come on, Lydia. Del told you a lot of things. You probably know more about the business than I do."

Lydia smiled briefly, and then the smile faded. "I don't think he did," she said. "At least, he didn't mention it."

"Are you sure?"

"No, of course not. He didn't say he was taking it with him, so I imagine he left it behind. Why? What's so important…"

"If he didn't take it with him, it's missing."

"Oh?"

I nodded, and Lydia dropped the stat on the piano, as if it had suddenly grown hot in her hand.

"How do you know?" she asked.

"It's not in the safe."

She fell silent, and the only sound in the room was the intake of her breath as she drew in on her cigarette. At last, she said, "This is all very good, Josh. A nice play. Trouble is, I don't believe a goddamned word of it."

"You still think…"

"I still think. I think, but I'm known as Charlie the Clam in some circles. I think, but I keep my mouth shut. I'm a smart girl, Josh." She walked to the coffee table, leaned over to put out the cigarette. The halter sprang out from her breasts, showing smooth whiteness where her tan ended. I wondered why she'd come all the way to the coffee table when there was an ashtray right behind her on the piano.

"You've got it all wrong, honey. I may not have loved Del, but he was my partner, and our business was doing fine."

"We agree then," she said.

"We agree about what?"

"I didn't love Del, either."

I felt my eyebrows go up.

"That really amazes you, doesn't it, Josh?"

"Well, I…"

"It shouldn't," she said coldly. "I told you I'm a smart girl. I

know which side my toast is buttered on, Josh. I like this apartment; I'd like to keep it."

"You're a little too fast for me, Lydia."

"Am I?" She took a step closer to me, and there was a small
smile on her mouth. She wore no lipstick, and her lips looked
raw and swollen. "Del provided this," she said. She swept her
arm backward, and the halter bobbed with the sudden motion.
"Del's gone now."

I was beginning to sweat, and I knew damned well the place
was air-conditioned. "So?"

"The partnership dissolves. And the surviving partner is free
to start another business."

"Me?" I asked again.

"No, Josh. Me."

She was very close now, close enough so that I could smell
the faint scent on her body. I looked into her eyes, and they
were hard and calculating, like the eyes of a whore I'd met in
Panama when I was in the Army. Just like that, and I half expected her to ask for the two bucks first. I hadn't enjoyed the
Panamanian wench—I'd reeled out of her cubby-hole feeling
dirty. And I wasn't enjoying Lydia now. She gave me that same
unclean feeling.

"I appreciate the offer," I started, "but…"

I didn't get a chance to say more. She stopped my mouth.
She stopped it efficiently with a kiss that was as calculated as
the glint in her eyes. I returned the kiss because I've never been
one to look at a gift mouth. There was more than the kiss. Lydia
owned a body, and she knew she owned one, and she did her
damnedest to make sure I knew it, too. She pulled away from
me suddenly, then, as if I'd tried to steal a kiss from her behind
the barn, fluttered her eyelashes girlishly, swallowed a breathless
little gasp, and backed away, her hand moving to her hair.

"Well!" she said. Her voice caught in her throat, and she successfully conveyed the impression of having gotten more than she bargained for. She was a shrewd, talented bitch, all right—but "Panama" was stamped on her shoulder.

"Well what?" I asked.

"Well, stay awhile, Josh." Her voice lowered on this, holding all the invitation of a black widow spider curling a leg at its mate.

I smiled.

"It *must* be the heat," I said. "More damn propositions in one day…" I shook my head sadly. "No dice, Lydia. Not now."

She raised one eyebrow. "No dice, Josh?" Her voice was smiling but her mouth was not.

"Sorry. A nice pitch—one of the nicest. I'm just not in the market."

"Maybe later. I'm Charlie the Clam, remember?"

"That would be effective blackmail, Lydia. *If* I'd killed Del. I didn't."

Lydia's mouth smiled now. "Maybe later, Josh," she repeated.

"Sure." I nodded. "Maybe."

I started for the door, and she called, "Don't forget this stat, Josh."

"Oh, Jesus!" I walked back to the center of the room, and she swept the stat from the piano and handed it to me.

"'Bye, Josh." Her voice rose on my name.

"So long, Lydia."

I walked out into the corridor and reached into my back pocket for my wallet. Lydia's door closed gently behind me, and I felt a sudden pang of regret for not having stayed with her. I shrugged that aside, folded the stat carefully, and was putting it into my wallet when the building fell on my head.

I dropped the stat and the wallet both, started to pitch forward

when the second blow caught me on the side of my face. I felt
my eardrum pop, saw the carpeted floor come up at me too
damned fast, and then my nose ploughed up three inches of
rug and somebody's heavy foot did its best to push my cheek-
bone out through my mouth.

My cheek exploded in a yellow burst of pain, and then little
yellow bubbles drifted across the top of my skull, turned to
purple, brown, black. They all flooded together, like black pebbles being sucked down a drain, and the blackness swirled
faster and faster until my consciousness went down the drain
with the pebbles.

The carpet was green.

This was a remarkable feat of deduction, considering the
fact that the carpet was a half inch from my face.

I pushed myself to my knees, remarking at the vividness of
the green. Almost like Lydia's eyes. It occurred to me that my
complexion was probably the same color, and then I remembered
the size 12 1/2 that had tried to kick my head into a corner. I put
my hand to my face. It came away red.

The red was sticky and warm. It made me ill, and I held my
guts together, trying not to retch. I struggled up to my feet,
wondering who had stolen the bones that were supposed to be
in my legs. I leaned against the wall, trying to gather strength
for the long, long journey to Lydia's door down the hall. After a
while, I started the trek, leaving a smudged trail of red on the
wails as I groped at them with my blood-stained hand in inef-
fectual attempts to steady myself. I reached Lydia's apartment
and rammed my palm against the chime panel.

I listened to the four chimes and I waited, and I pushed again,
and the chimes sounded melodiously, and I kept pushing and
hearing the beautiful chimes and waiting, and then it occurred

to me that there were probably two entrances to the apartment, and Lydia could very easily have left by the other one without ever having to step into the hallway to find me necking with the rug.

The thought was not a particularly cheering one. I wheeled for the elevators, stabbed at the weaving button on the wall, and waited for the car. I remembered my wallet, then, and started down the hall once more, bending over when I spotted it on the carpet. The bend started the New York Philharmonic on *The Anvil Chorus*, but I retrieved the wallet and began looking for the stat. It wasn't on the rug and it wasn't in the wallet, and I realized abruptly that I no longer owned a single copy of the Cam Stewart agreement.

I went back to wait for the elevator.

Quite curiously, I wanted to see Detective Sergeant Di Luca.

5.

The German High Command in the elevator and in the lobby did not like the looks of my bloodied face. They stared at me down their noses when I asked if they'd seen Miss Rafney leave, and they finally told me they had. Their attitude made it plain that people with bleeding cheekbones did not usually frequent these hallowed halls.

I pretended my cheek was a chronic bleeder, ignored their icy stares and tones, and found my way through the lobby and out into the street. By the time I'd reached a candy store, I'd already wiped most of the blood from my face, so the proprietor didn't give me a second look when I headed for the phone booth.

I dialed rapidly, waited while the phone rang, and then heard a rasping voice say, "Homicide, Sergeant Julian."

"Sergeant Di Luca, please."

"Moment."

When Di Luca came on, he was talking to someone else in the background. He shouted a parting word, then turned his voice to the phone. "Di Luca."

"Josh Blake. Have you got a moment?"

"All the time in the world."

"May I come down?"

"Sure. Did you find another body?"

"Not quite."

"All right, I'll be waiting for you."

"See you."

I hung up, caught a cab, and was walking into Di Luca's office fifteen minutes later. He stood up when I walked in, but he didn't extend his hand. He extended his eyes instead, and they raked over the cut on my cheek.

"Who slugged you?" he asked

"That's what I'd like to know."

"Where'd you get it?"

"In the hallway, outside Lydia Rafney's apartment."

"What were you doing there?"

"I wanted to find out if she knew whether or not Del took that agreement with him."

"Did she know?"

"Yes. She doesn't think he did. That's why I'm here."

"Why?"

"Whoever dented my head took the second copy of the agreement."

"That's interesting. Have a seat."

"Thanks, I'll stand."

"What else did she have to say?"

"Lydia?"

"Yes."

"Nothing." I paused. "Doesn't that mean anything to you? The fact that I was slugged? The fact that someone swiped the only remaining copy of the agreement? Doesn't that ring a bell?"

"Ring a bell? It starts a whole symphony, Mr. Blake."

"It damn well should. Seems to me it narrows things down considerably."

"How so?" Di Luca asked.

"There are only so many people who are interested in that agreement and the power it gives the agency."

"And who are these interested parties?"

I looked at Di Luca, trying to see whether or not he had his tongue in his cheek. It was hard to read any expression on that face of his. I sucked in a breath and said, "Rutherford, for one. He's Stewart's Hollywood agent. Without the Gilbert and Blake agency in the picture, he could make any movie deal he wanted to. But that agreement gives us TV rights, and his hands are tied as long as we've got those."

"So you figure he may have killed your partner to get the first copy, and then slugged you to get the second. That sounds logical. Shall we arrest him?"

"Are you being smart, Di Luca?"

"No, I'm being attentive. Who's your next murder suspect?"

He was beginning to make me feel foolish, but I went on anyway. "David Becker. He's the producer who wants the Cam Stewart properties. He'd give his right arm for them, in fact. He's anxious to close this deal, and if the agreements were missing, he'd have clear sailing—without a lot of bickering between agents. Besides, he's not anxious to give me twenty-five percent of his movie profits, which is what I want."

"And your third suspect?"

"The author, Cam Stewart. We've never met, but there's a goodly chunk of cash involved here, and everyone likes the smell of money. With that agreement out of the way, the deal would go through quickly, and a pile of cash would pour into the dusty coffers."

"Mmmm," Di Luca commented.

"What does that mean?"

He shrugged. "The same thing your theories mean. Nothing. I don't buy complicated murder motives. I don't buy everyone getting so het up over a lousy movie deal. I don't buy murder for a piece of paper. It's implausible, Blake. If it came in from one or your authors, you'd toss it into the wastebasket."

"Haven't you ever had a case that didn't go according to the way you wanted it?"

"Once," Di Luca admitted. "An ax murder. I thought it was the husband. It turned out to be the janitor, because the broad had spurned his advances. A simple motive. Right down the line. The motives are always simple, Blake. You come up with a bunch of crap, and I'm supposed to round everyone up and start looking for an elusive scrap of paper. Cloak and dagger stuff, the missing plans, the secret plot to blow up the Treasury Building." He shook his head. "No, Blake. I'm not buying."

"What are you buying?"

"That depends. For example, what did you do last night?"

"Why?"

"The dead man was your partner. Your hands still aren't clean."

"I was home."

"Alone?"

"No."

"With whom?"

"A girl."

"Lydia Rafney?"

"No."

"Did you know she was shacking with Del?"

"No."

"Then why'd you go to see her this morning?"

"I told you. I thought she might know about the agreement."

"Why should she know? Was she a silent partner?"

"No."

"Wasn't it because she was very close to Del? So close that they shared the same bed?"

"I never asked her."

"I did," Di Luca said drily. "There's no secret about it, Blake. She admitted it freely. So why are you trying to protect her maidenly purity?"

"I'm not. All right, she was shacking with Del. What difference does that make?"

"None. Except that Del was out of town last night, and you were home. You still haven't told me whom you were with."

"A girl. I forget her name."

"Lydia Rafney?"

"I answered that one already."

"It wasn't Lydia Rafney?"

"No."

"Was it Gail Gilbert?"

"Hell, no."

"Did Mrs. Gilbert know about her husband's little affair?"

"I'm sure I don't know."

"Did she or didn't she?"

"Why don't you ask her?"

"I will," Di Luca snapped. "What time did you get into the office this morning?"

"Nine-thirty."

"Who was there?"

"Everyone but Lydia."

"Where was she?"

"How would I know?"

"Didn't you check? Your receptionist said you asked her to call Lydia's home."

"I did."

"Was she there?"

"No."

"Where was she?"

"I don't know. The switchboard operator there said she was on her way to the office."

"What time did she get in?"

"About ten, I guess."

"Exactly?"

"I don't know. I didn't look at my watch."

"Why not?"

"I'd found Del a few minutes earlier. I still wasn't thinking clearly. What the hell difference does it make what time a secretary walks in?"

"You seemed disturbed about that when you asked your receptionist to call her."

"That was before I found Del dead."

"What time did you find him?"

"About nine-forty or so, I suppose."

"Did you look at a clock then?"

"No."

"What did you do?"

"I buzzed Tim Kennedy and asked him to come into Del's office."

"Why?"

"Because I was confused. I didn't know what to do."

"And then what?"

"Then I called the police."

"Before or after Lydia Rafney came in?"

"Before, I think. No, it was after. She was there when the call went through."

"You said she came in at ten."

"About that time."

"Your call here was clocked in at nine-fifty-three."

"All right, she came in a little earlier than ten."

"Seven minutes earlier, to be exact. Why'd you pick on ten o'clock as her time of arrival?"

"I didn't pick on anything. I just thought she came in at ten."

"Was she supposed to come in at ten?"

"She's supposed to come in at nine."

"Yes, but on this particular morning, was she supposed to come in at ten?"

"She's supposed to be there at nine every morning."

"Is she usually?"

"No."

"Then why were you so angry about it this morning?"

"Circumstances. That pesty writer, I wanted her to help me get rid of him."

"Are you usually sore when she comes in late?"

"Not unless something important is up."

"Have you ever bawled her out about lateness before?"

"No."

"Why not?"

"I just haven't."

"Because you knew she was shacking with Del?"

"Maybe."

"Yes or no."

"Yes, I guess so."

"You didn't want to offend Del, is that it?"

"I suppose you could say that."

"Then why'd you bawl her out this morning? Weren't you worried about offending Del anymore?"

"I told you…"

"Or did you know Del was dead, that he was beyond offending? Is that why you bawled her out?"

I suddenly realized that Di Luca had effectively led the conversation to the point where I was admitting I'd had angry words with Lydia. That hadn't been the case at all. I'd been sore, but when she finally did arrive at the office, I hadn't mentioned her lateness at all.

"I didn't bawl her out," I said. "You know I didn't."

"Sure, I know." Di Luca grinned boyishly. "Why don't you go home, Mr. Blake? I'll think about what you've told me. Maybe we'll look up these characters."

"Thanks," I said drily.

"I like you, too."

I got up and stalked out of his office, slamming the door

behind me. I felt drained, as if my brain had been picked clean by vultures. That lousy son of a bitch! He'd given me a grilling, and he'd made me look silly as hell; and worse, he'd even made me *feel* guilty.

It was hotter in the street now. Thinking about the heat in New York did not make me any cooler. For the second time that day, I wanted to be back in my apartment with a cool drink in my hand, and my backside immersed in a tub of water. I might even try immersing my backside in a cool drink, and forget the water completely. The idea appealed to me immensely. The thought of ice cubes bouncing off my naked torso was an ingenious one.

I thought of Gail Gilbert and her naked torso. That thought didn't help the heat any. So I switched back to thinking about the ice cubes again. I thought of those for a little while, trying to hail a cab, while the heat tried to parboil my brain. When I got the cab, I leaned back and gave the driver my address. Then I started thinking about Gail again.

I'd really treated her in a most cavalier manner. Actually, she hadn't deserved such a brush-off, especially not after what had happened to Del. I cursed myself for a slob, and a boor, and the worst kind of an idiot, and by the time I reached my apartment I was ready to call her and kiss her feet.

I opened the door, ripped off my shirt and trousers, mixed a cool Tom Collins, and then dialed her number, a Yonkers exchange. The phone rang three times before she lifted the receiver.

"Hello." Her voice was soft.

"Gail? This is Josh."

I'd been worrying about the heat until then, but the temperature of her voice suddenly transported me to Siberia. "Yes, what is it?"

"I...I felt I owe you an apology."

"Isn't that nice."

"I'm sorry about what happened, Gail, I..."

"I am, too. Let's Just forget it."

"No, really, Gail. I behaved rather poorly, I'm afraid, and..."

"Excuse me, Josh," she said coldly. "There's someone at the door."

"I'll hold on," I told her.

I heard the receiver clatter as she put it down on the table. I even heard her heels clicking as they moved away from the phone. I didn't hear anything then, so I sat back to wait, the phone in one hand, and the Tom Collins in the other.

The drink was cool. I sipped at it leisurely, thanking the powers that be for allowing Mr. Collins to invent such a wonderful little heat chaser, I sipped some more.

And I waited.

I took a big gulp, and another big gulp, and pretty soon the drink was gone, so I fished into the glass for the cherry I'd thoughtfully included. It took me a little while to get the cherry since I had the use of only one hand. I finally got it, though, and I chewed it and swallowed it, and then I remembered I was holding the phone with my other hand.

"Gail?" I asked.

There was no answer.

I glanced at my watch. Good God, she'd been gone for more than five minutes already!

"Gail!" I shouted.

I thought of Del Gilbert lying dead in his office. And I thought of the beating I'd taken in the hallway of Lydia's building. A tight panic crowded my chest

"Gail! Gail!"

There was no answer.

6.

I called her name once more, and then I hung up quickly. I snatched the receiver from its cradle almost immediately, and dialed Di Luca's number. The same cop I'd had earlier came on.

"Homicide, Sergeant Julian."

"Di Luca, please. And hurry."

"Sam," the sergeant called. "Some bug in a hurry."

Di Luca took the phone and said, "Di Luca speaking."

"This is Josh Blake again."

"Hello, Blake," he said dully.

"I'll get to the point, Di Luca. I was just talking to Gail Gilbert on the phone. She left the phone to answer the door. She never came back to the phone."

"How long was she gone?" Di Luca asked.

"More than five minutes."

"Maybe she forgot about you."

"I doubt it."

"So?"

"I think you'd better get to Yonkers damned fast."

He surprised me. I expected a long argument and perhaps a harangue, but Di Luca obviously recognized the potential danger as well as I did. "I'll get right over," he said.

"Will you call me when you get there?"

"All right."

"I'll stay by the phone."

"So long." He clicked off, and I held the dead receiver for a moment before putting it back into the cradle. I was worried. I was really worried now. You can take one murder in your stride, without losing much sleep over it, and you can laugh about a comparatively minor slugging. When the thing begins spreading, though, it's time to worry. It's time to start chewing things over—chewing them hard.

And there were a lot of things that needed chewing.

Like Del's reason for hieing back to the city and going straight to the office.

Why the hell would he do a thing like that?

Lots of reasons, sure. Like what?

Like a hot manuscript that needed immediate marketing. So Del left a big deal in Connecticut to rush home, when Tim or I or even Lydia could handle it perfectly well.

No, not a hot property. Our hottest property at the moment was Cam Stewart.

Maybe his business in Connecticut was finished. That was logical enough. He'd closed the deal, maybe, saw no reason to stick around any longer, and came back home.

But why go to the office?

Why not back to his own apartment, and his loving wife, Gail? Or why not over to Lydia's place? Why the office, and what the hell was he doing at the safe when he got it?

And how did the murderer know he'd be at the office, unless the murderer followed him all the way from Connecticut? Or unless Del came into the office and surprised the murderer there? But Di Luca said the shots had been fired from the door. It didn't sound likely that the murderer had been there before Del arrived.

I tried a mental picture for size.

Murderer at safe. Desk lamp on. Hears someone outside putting key into lock. Gets up, ducks into reception room, leaving safe open. Del comes in, goes into his office, sees open safe.

Murderer comes to door, shoots him, takes agreement he was looking for.

Except: 1) Would a murderer, or thief, or both, run out *towards* the newcomer? Chances are, he'd have ducked behind the desk or the couch, and taken his pot shots from there. He certainly would not go out to the reception room. 2) Wouldn't a murderer snap off the desk lamp when he heard someone coming?

Del was shot from the door. The desk lamp was on. The shots were fired hastily. I couldn't buy the murderer being there already. Del was followed, straight up to the office; and he was shot while looking for something in the safe, or while putting something back into the safe.

So who?

That was the big question. Who followed Del back from Connecticut? And why did Del go to the office?

I chewed it over a bit more, and I came up with a fat zero. I wondered what luck Di Luca was having, and I looked at the phone like a teenager on Saturday afternoon, praying for it to ring.

Suppose Gail had been done away with, too? What did that leave? A wanton murderer, someone killing for kicks? I couldn't buy that, either. Both copies of the Cam Stewart agreement were missing.

I looked at the phone again, and I thought of Gail once more, and my hands began to tremble. I wanted to get the hell out of the apartment and over to her place, but I'd told Di Luca I'd wait, and considering his temper, that would be the best plan to follow.

I mixed another Tom Collins, but it didn't taste as good as the first one I'd had. I swallowed it quickly, then poured a hooker of gin over the remaining ice, and downed that, too. The phone still had not rung.

I walked to the window, parted the limp curtains, and looked out over the sweltering city. A hell of a time for murder. A time for fun, the summer, a time for beach parties and short-lived romances. Not a time for Death.

Where the hell was Di Luca's call?

I began to think the worst. If everything had been all right, he'd have called by now. I formed a mental picture of Gail lying on the floor with a bullet in her head, twisted and crooked, the way Del had been. The picture got clearer, and I couldn't take it any longer. I went to the closet and was taking out a clean sports shirt when the phone rang. I dropped the hanger and the shirt and ran across the room. I lifted the receiver before the instrument had completed its first ring.

"Hello," I said anxiously.

"Josh?" the voice asked. I recognized the voice, and a flood or relief swept over me.

"Yes, Gail?"

"Josh, what on earth? I went to the door to get my groceries, and then went over the list with the boy. The next thing I know, there are policemen banging on the door. For goodness sake…"

"Give me that phone," I heard another voice say.

I waited, and then the voice said, "What the hell are you trying to pull, Blake?" It was Di Luca.

"Nothing. I thought…"

"You thought nuts! What's the grand idea? You think the police have nothing to do but chase around the city after dames taking in their groceries?"

"Look, Di Luca…"

"No, you look, Blake. Get the hell out of my hair! I'm trying to get a little work done on a homicide case, Every time you call or drop around, it sets me back another week. I'm tired of it, do you understand?"

"Look, I had no idea the grocery boy…"

"You're not paid to have ideas," Di Luca snapped. "I'm running that end of the show. That's my job. That's why I'm here. You just take care of your goddamned agency, and leave the murders to me."

"You finished, Di Luca?"

"I'm finished, yes!"

"Then listen to me. If you'd have found Gail Gilbert with her brains leaking out on the floor, you'd have been stamped into the sidewalk by every newspaper in town. You're damned lucky she's alive, and you're just sore because I was the one who told you something you should have known all along, that anyone connected with Del in any way is in possible danger."

"And you most of all, Blake. Unless you stop annoying me. So help me, I'll slam you into the can on a charge of obstructing justice! Now get the hell out of my hair, Blake!"

I was ready to shout back at him when Gail came on the phone again. "Josh?"

"Yes. Look, Gail, I'm sorry about all this. I got worried when you didn't come back to the phone, and I thought…well, I guess I'm a little jumpy after what happened."

"I understand, Josh."

"Just forgive me for this, and for the way I acted earlier, will you?"

Her voice brightened. "Sure, Josh."

"And give Sherlock a fat kick in the keister for me."

Gail giggled, and then said, "He'll hear you."

"The hell with him. I'll be seeing you, Gail."

"All right."

"So long."

I hung up, still fuming over the brush with Di Luca. I mixed another Tom Collins, and this time I enjoyed it, and when I bit into the cherry at the end of the drink, I pretended it was Di Luca's head. You leave a murder case in the hands of an orangutan, and the results were likely to be astonishing. He'd probably be out chasing the janitor of the office building soon, simply because a janitor had once figured largely in a case he'd had. Simple motives! My foot! With two important agreements missing, and with one partner dead, and the other slugged to get those agreements. Simple motives! What the hell could be simpler than that?

But why did Del go to the office?

The goddamn question kept hounding me, and I wondered if someone else might have the answer to it. Gail?

Hardly. Del told her practically nothing, and I doubted if she knew anything at all about the Cam Stewart deal

Lydia? Now that was a horse of a different color. I went to the closet again, pulled out the fresh shirt and a pressed pair of trousers, and dressed hastily. Perhaps she'd be home by now, and perhaps she knew.

I locked up and walked down to the street, deciding against using the car. Lydia's place was about five minutes from mine, and with all the heat, I preferred walking rather than going through the routine of getting the car from the garage and driving.

The German High Command had wilted slightly from the heat when I reached the building. I headed for the switchboard. The Army there had fared better, aided by the air-conditioning system.

"Miss Rafney," I said. "Has she returned yet?"

"Yes, sir," the man said.

"Ring her, will you? Tell her Mr. Blake is here again."

The switchboard operator rang, and then took the earphones from his head. "There's no answer, sir," he said.

"Mmm. All right if I go up anyway?"

"Well…"

"I was here before. You remember me."

"Well, it's not really permissible, sir, but I suppose…"

"Thank you."

I took the elevator up to Lydia's floor and rang the bell outside her apartment, listening to the four chimes sound inside. I rang again. There was no answer.

I tried the knob, figuring her to be taking a nap or something, or perhaps lounging in the bathtub, which was as good a place to be as any in this weather. I kicked around the idea of joining her. The door opened when I twisted the knob.

"Lydia?" I called.

When I got no answer, I shrugged and headed through the living room, and toward the bathroom, guessing at the closed doors. I knocked on one and said, "Lydia?"

No answer.

I knocked on another, and it opened under the force of my knuckles, swinging wide, slowly, slowly.

The room was a bedroom. It was a very nice bedroom, with satin sheets, all monogrammed with the letter L in a large diamond. The diaphanous curtains at the window hung limply. The window was open, but there wasn't the faintest hint of a breeze. There was a dresser arrangement flanking both sides of the window, with mirrors that looked like extensions of the window itself. A box of powder was open on the dresser top. A brush and a comb lay near the powder puff.

Lydia Rafney lay on the floor near the dresser, two bullet holes in her head.

I looked at the blood on her face, and then my eyes traveled the length of her body. She was still in street clothes, a seersucker suit that she wore with the perfection of a mannequin. The jacket was still buttoned. She wore high-heeled shoes, no stockings. Her skirt had hiked up over her thighs when she fell. She wore no slip.

Her body looked alive and warm. The holes punched in her face told me she was very dead.

I passed my hand over my eyes. Finding corpses didn't appeal to me. They hit me in the gut with the force of sledge hammers. I shook my head blankly and walked out of the bedroom. I walked through the living room and out of the apartment, and over to the elevators. I buzzed for a car, and when it came, I stepped in, and it took me down to the lobby. I walked through the lobby and then out of the building. It was like walking into the mouth of a blast furnace.

I walked past the front of the building, around the corner. I stopped, waited for a car to pass, and then crossed the street. The sun beat down on my head and shoulders, and I kept seeing Lydia with the holes in her head, and the skirt pulled up over her thighs.

I'd have to call the police. Yes, I'd have to do that. Yes.

I turned and headed back for the building. I'd ask one of the men in the lobby if I could use their switchboard. I blinked my eyes, but the picture of Lydia persisted.

I heard the sirens, and I blinked against the sun, and wondered who had found the body and called the police. I stopped in front of the building as the white-topped car pulled to the curb. A patrolman opened the door nearest the curb and stepped out. I watched as he went into the lobby. I debated going after him, decided to stay out of it until I was needed. I hailed a cab and went back to my own apartment.

Another prowl car was waiting for me when I arrived. I paid the cabbie and started for the lobby, and a cop walked up to me swiftly.

"Mr. Blake?"

"Yes."

"Want to come along with us?"

"All right," I said dully.

He led me to the car, held the door open while I squeezed in beside the driver. He got in, closed the door behind him, and we started off, heading west.

Go West, young man, I thought. Into the arms of Hopalong Di Luca.

I wasn't wrong. They brought me to the precinct house, and Di Luca was waiting. He tapped a pencil on his desk, eyed me carefully, and said, "Lydia Rafney is dead."

"I know," I said.

"The elevator men said they took you up to her apartment."

"I was there," I said. "She was dead when I got there."

"That's your story. Why'd you go there?"

"I thought she might know why Del went straight to the office on his return to the city."

"Did she?"

"I didn't get a chance to ask her. She was dead when I arrived."

"You're always mighty handy when a corpse turns up, aren't you?"

"If we had a good cop on the case, maybe there wouldn't be as many corpses."

"Maybe you should join the force."

"Maybe I should."

"What time did you allegedly find her, Blake?"

"I didn't look at my watch."

"Were you around when the prowl car arrived?"

"Yes."

"Why didn't you report the murder immediately?"

"I was dazed."

"Oh, come off it!"

"I was! I walked around for a few minutes, and then realized I should report it. I headed back for the building, and that's when the cops pulled up."

"Why didn't you tell them your story?"

"I figured you'd get around to me soon enough. I don't like telling the same story ten times over."

"And she was dead when you arrived, huh?"

"Yes."

"That's the way you tell it. Would you like to hear my version?"

"Sure."

"All right, read it and weep. You called Gail Gilbert. She left the phone to get her groceries, and you suddenly got an idea. You hung up, called me, and sent me scooting over there while you told me you'd be waiting by your phone for my call. It's about five minutes from your place to Lydia Rafney's. All right, Blake, suppose you didn't wait by the phone for my call? Suppose you figured that would be a very nice little alibi? Suppose you slipped out, put two slugs in your sweetheart's face…"

"She wasn't my sweetheart!"

"…two slugs in your sweetheart's face, and then ran back to your own apartment, getting there in time to take my call. As far as I could tell, you were sitting by that phone every minute of the time."

"That's just where I was."

"That's where you *say* you were. I say you may have been with Lydia, and I say you may have shot her to death, and I say I'm booking you on suspicion of murder!"

"What? You're nuts, Di Luca, Even if your crazy theory were right, why the hell would I go back to Lydia's place? You're being downright ridiculous!"

Di Luca smiled. "Haven't you read enough mysteries to know, Blake? The murderer *always* returns to the scene of his crime."

"Stop mouthing platitudes at me, Di Luca. You know damn well I had nothing to do with Lydia's death."

"I'm booking you, Blake."

"Why? Because you don't like me? Because your cop's ego is hurt? Because you should have taken better care of Lydia in the first place? Is that why?"

"Don't be a kid, Blake. I'm booking you because you're a suspect and I'm a cop. If you're clean, we'll find out soon enough. We'll let you go then. But only if you're clean."

"Sure, go ahead. Book me. You've got a murderer running around loose somewhere out there, but you book *me*. You're a smart cop, Di Luca. They should have you handing out license plates, or collecting tolls on the Whitestone Bridge."

"Watch it, Blake."

"You know what false arrest is, Di Luca?"

"I know."

"So does my lawyer. Lock me up, smart guy. We'll see how long you stay in plainclothes."

"We'll see," Di Luca said.

"Where's your phone?"

"In the hallway, if you want privacy. Or you can use the one on my desk. Make it fast, Blake."

"Why? What's the big rush?"

Di Luca's smile broadened. "You're right, Blake. No rush at all. You'll be here all night, anyway."

7.

It was going to be another lulu, and Di Luca's jail had at least been cool.

He'd had to let me go, of course, and he did so reluctantly and only after the facts began piling up against him. The facts added up like this:

a) A paraffin test (which Di Luca claimed was notoriously unreliable) showed no trace of powder dots on either of my palms.

b) In spite of the weather (and in spite of the coroner's reluctance to go out on a limb in a gun-wound case), rigor mortis had already set in when the police found Lydia's body. If I *had* killed her while Di Luca was out chasing after Gail, the body would still have been warm. The coroner indicated that the shooting had taken place from within one to two hours before the discovery of the body, and death was instantaneous.

c) This still did not clear me in Di Luca's eyes. I could very well have killed Lydia the *first* time I visited her, except for a few other facts. Chief among these was the fact that Lydia had left her building before I did, the first time I went there. The German High Command corroborated this. They had seen her leave. She was, at least, still alive when I finally picked myself off the carpet and left the building.

d) The German High Command also reported that they had seen Lydia returning, about twenty minutes after I'd left. This placed me in Di Luca's office at about that time, so I could not have killed her then.

The switchboard operator told Di Luca that Lydia's apartment had not answered his ring when I'd gone there the second time. They had seen her return, and knew she was home. They allowed me to go up because they recognized me from my previous visit. Her failure to answer the phone seemed to substantiate the fact that she was already dead when I arrived. And even Di Luca realized I'd have used the service entrance and elevators (as the murderer had undoubtedly done) if I'd been bent on murder.

So, I hadn't killed Lydia.

I'd known that all along, of course. It was with relief that I greeted the police acknowledgment of the fact, but that still didn't tell anyone who *did* kill her. Or why.

I went down to my garage and picked up the Buick. The sun hadn't turned on all its wattage yet, and I figured driving wouldn't be too bad. And it would be best to make any visits I wanted to make right now, while the pavements were still comparatively cool. Del lived—or had lived—in Yonkers, and I could never figure why he'd set up house for Lydia in Manhattan, unless he worked on the theory that it was best not to romp in your own back yard.

Del's home was not a pretentious affair. It was a simple shingle and brick job, ranch style, with a batch of mountain laurel and rhododendron on either side of the low, brick front stoop. White bamboo drapes were closed over the long picture window of the living room, fronting half of the house. An ivy-covered and shrub-hidden fence extended from the right side of the house, and a red plastic hose was unwound in the yard, trailing over the slightly browned grass like a long snake. A lawn mower rested against the fence, and I wondered if Gail Gilbert had been out gardening before I'd arrived. I climbed the brick steps and pressed my finger against the square panel in the door jamb. I heard a buzzer sounding behind the closed door, but no one answered it. I opened the screen door and tried the big brass knob on the wooden door. It was locked.

I walked to the side of the house, using the slates imbedded in the grass, and climbed the steps leading to the kitchen door. The blinds were drawn, but I pushed the buzzer there anyway, and still got no answer. I saw the milk boxes on the porch then, lifted the cover of one, and saw the moist bottom of the box. Well, at least the milkman had been here, and Gail had taken in the milk. She hadn't stayed out all night, and considering her condition, that was a good thing.

I walked down to the Buick, looking back at the house once more. There was no sign of movement or life. I opened the door of the car, slid in behind the wheel, slammed the door shot, and then sat there for a few minutes. I lighted a cigarette and puffed on it idly. The mailman was just coming around. He glanced at me behind the wheel, then looked down at the letters in his hand, and walked right past Gail's house. I started the car, put down the top, and then drove off. I found a candy store, got change from the proprietor, and stepped into the closest phone booth.

I dialed the office, and the phone rang twice before Jeanette answered.

"Gilbert and Blake, good morning."

"Honey, this is Mr. Blake. How's it going?"

"Fine. Are you coming in, Mr. Blake?"

"Maybe later today. Is Tim in yet?"

"Yes, sir."

"Put him on, will you?"

"Just a moment, sir."

I waited a second or two, listening to the clicks of Jeanette's switchboard. Tim came on then.

"Hello, Josh."

"Morning, Tim. How's it going?"

"A little quiet, but all right. Are you coming in?"

"Later, maybe. Think you can hold the fort?"

"Sure."

"Fine. Listen, will you dig up Cam Stewart's address for me?"

"You going up there?"

"I thought it might be a good idea."

I waited, and then Tim came back with the address, and I jotted it down on one of the agency cards. "If anything important comes up, I'll be there, Tim. Anything you can't handle yourself."

"Okay. Fine."

"I'll see you."

"Right."

I waited until Tim hung up, and then I got out of the booth and had an egg cream at the counter. I went out to the Buick then and asked a passerby how to hit the Saw Mill River Parkway. He gave me complicated directions, and I thanked him and followed them, or tried to. I had to stop two more pedestrians before I finally found the parkway, but once on it I had clear sailing. I kept on it until I hit the Merritt Parkway, and that took me into Connecticut and Cam Stewart's town. It was a quiet town, lush with big shade trees and carefully landscaped lawns. I drove past the big white courthouse, the stone-faced churches with their high white steeples, the circle in the center of the town, with the bronze statue of a Revolutionary War hero in it. I kept driving past the town, out on a macadam road that wound through the countryside like a black snake. It was a pleasant drive, and I really enjoyed being away from the city. Big trees flanked the road, their branches arching overhead, the leaves rustling on the mild breeze. I thought of the thousand-window bakery that was New York City, and I was thankful to be away from the oven for even just a little while.

I was almost sorry I finally had to stop the car. The place was just around a wide curve in the road. I rounded the curve, spotted the pillars, and jammed on my brakes.

They stood on either side of a wide gravel driveway. They were both made of solid brick, painted white, and a rustic lamp was set into the top of each. The pillar on the left bore the wrought-iron legend, GUNSMOKE. The pillar on the right, lettered in the same wrought-iron script, simply said ACRES. Gunsmoke Acres.

Gunsmoke had been the title of Cam Stewart's first Western novel. It had been an instant smash, selling 20,000 copies in the hardcover edition, and going well over the two million mark in the paperbacks. That was a lot of mazoo, especially for a Western, which generally sold between 2,000 and 2,500 copies in the hardcover edition and something more than 150,000 in the paperbacks. Nor had that been the end of the road. There had been five novels since *Gunsmoke* and, if anything, the author's popularity had increased. Stewart's Westerns were packed with power, and loaded with authenticity. There were rumors that Stewart was raised on an Arizona ranch, had learned about the West and Westerners through direct contact. The counter-rumors stated that the author was the offspring of a Chinese missionary, and knew nothing at all about America, let alone the West.

The press hadn't got around to showing Stewart's picture on its front pages yet, but the press is notoriously slow when it comes to literary matters, unless a Nobel Prize is concerned. But Stewart was hot, and I was willing to bet my agency against a collar button that the next year—especially with a movie deal involved—would find the author's face plastered in every periodical. It takes a while for the wagon to get rolling, but once it does, everyone hops aboard for the free ride.

Gunsmoke Acres—the name was appropriate because the royalties on the first book alone had probably been enough to pay for the joint.

I slipped the car into reverse, backed out onto the road, and then pointed the nose up the gravel driveway. The wheels skidded when they hit the gravel, then took hold, and I started up the drive slowly.

The place had been *most* appropriately named, I discovered.

Gunsmoke. Everything about it was the color of gunsmoke, grey and white. The gravel itself was a sharp grey and the drive was lined with white birches. Silver maples and silver poplars spread out behind the birches, interspersed with Japanese black pine. Blue-green Andorra junipers crowded the pines, and heavy black boulders dotted the foliage lining the drive. The impression was one of smoke: greys and whites and blue-greens and blacks. The impression was also one of wealth because it must have taken three Japanese gardeners to keep the approach to the house looking that way.

The road continued for about half a mile, cutting in a leisurely way through the carefully landscaped approach. I rounded a bend then, and the house sprang into view.

It was one of those long, low jobs, the kind that need a half acre for the bedroom alone. It sprawled on the rise of a hill, and the sun glistened on its windowed walls. The house seemed to be all glass and stone. It had a long, flat roof, and windows covered most of the walls from roof to foundation line. The rest was fieldstone, and, for variety, redwood was used on the gable and as facing on either side of the entrance door. I don't know what I expected—possibly a corral and a bunk house. But this was strictly modern, the kind they call functional, the kind you find a lot of in California and warmer climates. It was certainly impressive. It was quietly regal, like a millionaire slipping a

waiter a ten-cent tip. It was slender and beautiful, poised, like
an ash blonde stepping out of a taxi. It was clean and trim, like
a new yacht with a good crew.

It was a *house,* by God, and it made my mouth water and it
made me want to close that goddamned deal as soon as possible. The gravel drive ran in a circle in front of the entrance
door, and then branched off to a two-car fieldstone garage set a
little way off in the woods. I followed the branch and parked
the Buick behind a black Caddy near the closed garage doors. I
got out and sniffed the air a little, and then started toward the
house.

The gravel scrunched underfoot, making a sound as clean
and as sharp as the house itself. The sound echoed in the silent
woods, and I took another deep breath and thought of related
items like luxury and undisturbed living, and money, and money,
and money.

The black wrought-iron knocker on the front door was a
twisted combination of Cam Stewart's initials and, curiously
enough, it looked amazingly like a dollar sign, I heard footsteps
inside, and then the door opened wide, and a hawk-faced gent
dressed in black peered out at me. His collar was high and stiff,
and he wore a black tie, and he looked like an undertaker on a
holiday, or a vulture at a cocktail party. He smiled, or leered, as
if he were measuring me for a coffin, and then politely asked,
"Yes, sir?"

"Cam Stewart," I said.

"Yes, sir, and whom shall I say is calling?"

"Mr. Blake. Joshua Blake."

"One moment, sir."

He closed the door, and I kept looking at the dollar sign Cam
Stewart's initials made. It was most attractive. I waited for a
good deal more than one moment, and then the door opened

again, and the undertaker tried his fiendish grin once more. I almost shivered.

"If you'll follow the flagstone path around to the back, sir," he said. "To the swimming pool."

"Thanks," I told him. He nodded, still grinning evilly, his eyes studying me with professional interest. I followed the gravel until it joined a flagstone path that ran around the side of the house opposite the garage. A troop of shrubs, bushes, and trees were lined up alongside the path, guaranteeing privacy. Considering the fact that the property probably stretched for a hundred acres or so, I wondered about the necessity for the green sentinels. Perhaps Stewart went in for sunbathing, or orgies, or some damn thing—and maybe the gardeners were curious. Well, I couldn't blame them. I was curious myself. I wanted to meet this best-selling writer. Probably resembled the horses in some of the Draw Hudson novels.

I rounded the corner of the house and my mouth fell open when I saw the swimming pool. It glistened a pale blue under the strong rays of the sun. It was amoeba-shaped, long and loose, sprawled out over the lawn. The water looked clean and cold, and I felt like sprinting across the lawn and taking a flying leap. I didn't.

I didn't because a guy and a girl were sitting in beach chairs by the pool. The girl had her back to me, and all I could see was her black hair curling down over her shoulders. The man was facing me, and whereas he didn't resemble a horse, the fine line of distinction almost eluded me. He wore thick eyeglasses, and they caught the sun as he lifted his head now, giving him a fiery-eyed appearance. The fierceness did not go with the rest of his face. It was a perfect circle, as round as a cue ball, and just as white. He had no hair on the smooth, white skin of his head. A fringe of black hugged each ear, but that was all. To make up for this serious lack, he had grown a big black mustache under his flat nose. The mustache looked like a rubber mat upon which the nose carelessly lounged. The thick lips beneath the mustache reached out for the highball glass he held in his hand. His black eyebrows shot up onto the stretch of skin that was his forehead and his scalp at the same time.

Cam Stewart, I thought. *Portrait of a Westerner.*

I was not disappointed. I'd long since stopped being surprised by the appearance of writers.

I smiled my best smile, extended my palm, and politely said, "Mr. Stewart?"

The bald guy eyed me curiously, and his brows shot up again. He blinked at me, and a small smile curled the edges of his heavy mustache.

"Mr. Stewart?" I asked again.

"I'm Cam Stewart."

The voice came from behind me. It was soft and throaty, and I whirled suddenly, surprised.

The brunette in the beach chair was wearing a bathing suit, if I may be allowed a little license. It was really a narrow white strip across her full breasts, and a shrunken white handkerchief slung over her waist. The suit was wet. It was very wet. It was so wet that it made me begin to perspire. It clung to everything it covered, and it did not cover very much.

I blinked and said, "I beg your pardon?"

"I'm Cam Stewart," the brunette said again.

"You…"

"Camelia Stewart," she said in that hushed voice of hers. "Cam Stewart, Mr. Blake."

I looked at Cam Stewart, and I recalled the vivid sex scenes that had tumbled head over keister from her typewriter. She was long, this girl, long and tawny, with skin the color of old bronze. She lounged in the beach chair barefoot, with her legs crossed, with the bathing suit soaking wet, with the curve of her hip ripe and full, with her breasts straining against the taut top of the suit. She smiled, and her lips were a cushiony red, and her eyes were a dark blue, almost black against the tan of her skin. She arched a black brow and tilted her head and the smile was a teasing one, as if she enjoyed shocking the trousers off of agents by telling them Cam Stewart was a woman.

I swallowed my Adam's apple and said, "I…I didn't know. I mean…"

"You expected a horse."

"Well, yes. I mean, no, hell no. I expected a man."

She smiled that lazy smile, and she began jiggling one foot. "And I'm not that," she said softly.

"No," I said, "you are not that."

She waved one hand languidly, the bright red fingernails glinting in the sun. "Mr. Blake," she said, "meet Dave Becker."

I took my eyes from her and turned my gaze to the moon-faced gent with the ivy under his nose.

"How do you do, Mr. Becker?" I said.

Becker grunted. "Fine."

His brows had pulled together into a deep scowl, and I gathered he didn't like me very much. Considering the fact that he was the producer who was moving heaven and earth to get his paws on the Stewart properties, and considering the fact that I was his chief opposition, his antagonism was not exactly unexpected.

We stood—or rather I stood while he sat—looking at each other for the space of about thirty seconds. Then Becker put down his drink, gripped the arms of his chair, and said, "So you're the chiseler."

"Oh, Dave," Cam said, covering her lips and allowing a shocked laugh to sneak through her fingers.

"He is, Cam," Becker said. "A stick-up artist, by Christ. A second-story man."

"That's enough," I said.

"Sure, that's enough. Sure. Sure." He nodded his head, sore as hell. Then he raised those black brows again, and his eyes studied my face for a few seconds. "What the hell do you want here, Blake?"

"My partner was killed," I said.

"Good," Becker said.

"We heard about it," Cam said. "A terrible thing."

"Yes."

"What was so terrible about it?" Becker wanted to know. "He was even a bigger crook than Blake."

"Listen, Becker," I said tightly, "how would you like to take a little swim?"

"Never mind," Becker said, waving his forefinger at me. "Don't start playing strong-arm. I'll tell you something, Blake. I just told it to Cam, and now I'll tell it to you. You listening?"

"I'm listening."

Becker nodded his head curtly. "All right. You say you got an agreement Cam Stewart signed. Okay, Cam says she never signed anything like it. She says…"

"What?" I turned to face Cam, and she shrugged rounded, browned shoulders.

"I really don't remember, Mr. Blake."

"Well, you damn well signed," I informed her. "You wrote a letter giving us sole and exclusive permission to handle radio and TV rights to every one of your books, provided we paid a five-hundred-dollar option. You signed that letter, and that makes it as good as gold, and our accountants have the cancelled check for the five bills. What kind of a snow job is this, anyway?"

Cam shrugged again. "I just don't remember."

"That's a shame, Miss Stewart. Something as important as that should be remembered."

"All right, smart guy," Becker said. "You say you got an option letter. How long does the option run?"

"You asked for it, smart guy. No time limit is stated in the letter of agreement. That means it runs indefinitely, smart guy."

"I'm from Missouri," Becker said sourly. "You got such a letter, then you produce it. Until that time, I'm dealing directly with Miss Stewart. The deal will go through without you, and you can damn well whistle. You got that, Blake? I'm not going to sit on something as big as this while some crook…"

I didn't wait for more. I yanked him out of the beach chair, and then I swung him around and grabbed the collar of his shirt and the seat of his pants. I propelled him toward the pool let him go just at the edge, with him yelling, "You bastard!" all the way. He spread his arms wide, and when he hit the water, it looked like Old Faithful on a clear day. Cam Stewart burst out with a delighted laugh. I stood on the edge of the pool, and she continued laughing until Becker surfaced and swam to a ladder. He climbed the ladder, stood there dripping wet, and shook his fist at me.

"Go ahead," he said, "make jokes. See how funny it is, later. Go ahead."

Cam covered her mouth, trying to stop the new flow of laughter, but she couldn't. I was glad she couldn't, because she really laughed heartily, and when she laughed she put everything she owned into it. She owned a lot, and although the bathing suit was almost dry now, it still didn't do much of a job. So she laughed, and she kept laughing, and I was tickled pink and ready to join her. Becker stormed off toward the house, and after a little while she stopped laughing.

"I'm sorry about your friend," I said.

"That's all right."

"I just don't like being called a crook."

"Especially when you are one."

"Now, listen…"

"I'm only teasing, Mr. Blake." She was.

"Then what's all this business about not remembering the letter of agreement?"

"I sign so many agreements," she said.

"And the five-hundred-dollar check?"

"I cash so many checks."

I grinned. "I'll bet you do."

"I do. Isn't it disgusting?"

"No," I said frankly.

She looked at me secretly. "It's not disgusting at all. It's the best damned thing that ever happened to me. You know what I was doing before I thought up Draw Hudson?"

"No. What?"

"Would you like a drink?"

"No, thanks. What were you doing before you dreamed up your cowboy?"

She giggled and covered her mouth again. "You won't believe it."

"I will."

"You say you will, but no one ever does."

"What were you doing?"

"Guess."

"Oh, for Pete's sake…"

"Go on, guess. I like to hear the answers."

I looked at her long body stretched out in the chair. "A model?"

"Oh, really. Christ, no. Me? A model?"

"You'd make a good model."

She chuckled again and sucked in a deep breath. "For bras, maybe. Go on, guess."

"For lots of things," I said, watching the curve of her leg and the flatness of her stomach.

"Guess," she insisted, ignoring my eyes.

"A schoolteacher?"

"Do I look like a schoolteacher?"

"Hell, no."

"What do I look like? Use your imagination."

"This is my third and last guess, yes?"

"All right, go on."

"A high-priced call girl."

I watched her eyes because I wasn't sure how she'd take this, but she laughed suddenly, that same hearty laugh that utilized all of her.

"Oh, God, is *that* what I look like?"

"No, not really. You tell me now."

"I worked in Brentano's."

"What?"

"See? You don't believe me."

"You mean you sold books?"

"Yes, sir. Not real books. I worked in the basement. I sold pocket-size books."

"I'll be damned. Westerns?"

"Westerns, mysteries, historical romances, everything. Hell, I read more than I sold."

"What did you read?"

"All of them. A few stood out in my mind. I read, and I read, and I read until I was red in the face. Then I decided to write one."

"*Voilà,* Draw Hudson!"

"No. *Voilà* Priscilla Masterson."

"Who?"

"The heroine of the first novel I wrote. She is now in the incinerator."

"And then came Draw Hudson."

"Yes. Then came Draw Hudson."

"How?"

"The milkman."

"What?"

"The milkman. He was long and lean, with grey eyes and thin lips. He had a deep tan from being outside so much, and he had a horse—a real horse—pulling his wagon. You very rarely see horse-drawn milk wagons anymore, but he had one. He called his horse Duke, though I think she was a mare."

"That's what Hudson calls his horse, isn't it?"

"Sure. Hudson is the milkman, but for Christ's sake, don't tell anyone."

"I don't believe you."

"You don't, huh? You should have seen that milkman. I bet he was responsible for more broken homes than the San Francisco Earthquake."

I laughed, hoping she'd join me, but she only smiled.

"So you took your milkman, sexed him up, gave him two six-guns, a batch of women ready to tumble into bed, and you revolutionized the Western."

"And," she added, "made a lot of money at it. Revolutions don't interest me, Mr. Blake…"

"Josh."

"Sure. They don't interest me. The farthest West I've been is New Jersey, where a guy took me to a burlesque in Union City. I don't crave the wide open spaces, and I hate the smell of horses. I deplore guns."

"All kinds?"

"Huh?"

".45's?"

"All kinds," she said. "There're only a few things I like, Josh, Just a few."

"And those?"

"Money."

"You're normal."

"Whiskey. In moderation."

"You're still normal. Is that all?"

She paused and smiled a quiet smile, looking up at me with devilish eyes. "My third is perfectly normal, too."

I cleared my throat. "I see."

She stuck her tongue in her cheek and nodded her head knowingly. "I thought you would." She paused then, leaned forward, and added, "I like you, Josh."

Her leaning forward had done devastating things to the top piece of her suit. My hands began to tremble a little on the arm of the chair.

"I like you, too," I said.

"Fine." She stood up, sucked in another breath and said, "I'm sorry all this garbage had to come up, Josh. I honestly don't remember signing any agreement, and I'll go along whichever way the deal works out."

"You can get into trouble, hon," I said. "Heaps of trouble."

"That's what your partner said." She shrugged. "I've got money enough to fight trouble. It doesn't bother me."

"Bad publicity…"

"Every one of my books has been panned. I'm still the hottest thing on the scene today." She paused. "Speaking in a literary sense."

"Of course."

"So, whichever way the wind blows, I bend with it. I like money, Josh. If Draw Hudson gets into the movies, I'll make money on the deal, and I'll also sell more books. I want him to get into the movies."

"How badly?"

"I don't follow."

"How badly? Badly enough to kill a man for it?"

Cam smiled. "All the killing I do is between the covers of my books."

"I'm glad to hear that."

"Want to take a swim, Josh?"

"I haven't a suit."

"There's probably one around the house. Come on, I'll see if we can't accommodate you."

She started for the flagstone path, and someone called, "Hey! Anybody home?"

"Goddamn it," Cam said. "This place is beginning to look like Grand Central Station." She turned to me, and her eyes narrowed. "We might have had a pleasant afternoon, Josh."

"Who is it?" I asked.

"From the tone of the bellow, I'd say it was Carlyle."

"Rutherford?"

"Mm."

"Another fellow who thinks I'm a crook," I said. "Maybe we'll have some more swimming, after all."

"Maybe not."

"Huh?"

"You've never met Carlyle, I take it."

"No."

"I wouldn't advise any wrestling. He's a big boy."

"The bigger…"

I stopped short because Carlyle Rutherford had swung into

view around the corner of the house. That is, he barged into view. Or, to be more accurate, he consumed the landscape, blotted the sky, overwhelmed the vicinity. He was a big boy, indeed. He was a very big boy. He measured an easy six-five from the flat soles of his canvas-topped shoes to the brown crew-cut that hugged his skull. He had massive shoulders, and a chest that came from weight-lifting. A loud sports jacket covered the shoulders and chest, and he wore an off-color orange sports shirt, buttoned at the throat. Tan gabardine slacks completed the outfit, and they went well with the ruddy California brown of his face. The face could have belonged to a football player, or a prize fighter. The nose had been bashed in, probably with a knee or a sledge hammer. The eyebrows were crooked. The lips were thin and merciless. The eyes were a deep, dark brown. It would not be wise to wrestle with him.

"Cam!" he whispered, and the trees shook, and the house rocked a little on its foundation. "Cam, you delectable piece, how are you?"

He rushed forward like a big grizzly, his arms outstretched, his fingers wide. He gathered Cam into his arms and hugged her tightly, and I thought he'd suffocate the poor girl. He dropped her finally, like a tree he had uprooted, and then noticed me for the first time. One of his crooked eyebrows shot up onto his brow, and he looked at Cam quizzically, waiting for an introduction.

"Josh Blake," Cam said after taking a deep breath. "Carlyle Rutherford."

"So," Rutherford said. I remembered the not-so-pleasant phone conversation we'd had yesterday, and I waited for more. He smiled, though, surprising me, and extended one of his large paws.

"How do you do?" I said, taking his hand and waiting for the bear squeeze. It didn't come. He pressed my hand firmly, and then let it go.

"You're a smart cookie, Blake," he said. "I admire smart businessmen."

"Thank you."

"I understand your partner handed in his jock."

"What?"

"Gilbert. Shot, wasn't he?"

"Yes."

Rutherford shook his head. "Shame. I understand he was even shrewder than you."

"He was shrewd, and she was nude…" Cam quoted.

Rutherford turned. "How's that?"

"He was shrewd, and she was nude," she repeated, a smile curling her crimson mouth. "She grew nuder and he grew shrewder. She grew nuder, and he grew shrewder, and he…"

Rutherford erupted in a booming laugh that threatened to start a landslide. He kept laughing, with his shoulders shaking, and his mouth wide open, and his head thrown back. When he finally got control of himself, he said, "Christ, what a witty piece."

"But forgetful," I said.

Rutherford shrugged. "Yeah, yeah," he said philosophically. "You're referring to the agreement again, eh, Blake?"

"The agreement," I said.

"You're a shrewd bastard, Blake," Rutherford said, the friendly smile still on his face. "I admire that, I told you so. You know when to hop onto a good thing, and I understand your late, lamented partner was wiser than Solomon. He's dead now, sure, but you're not lacking anything in the marbles department, I admire what you're trying to pull. If it comes off, you'll go down in history."

"I'm not trying to pull anything," I said.

"No?" Rutherford shrugged his huge shoulders. "Well, maybe not. Let's look at it this way, though. Ever since *Gunsmoke* was published, I've been breaking my back trying for a movie sale. I know that Hollywood jungle, Blake. I know it like my left ear lobe, and by Christ, I worked on this one. I broke my back, and also a few heads, and the doors all stayed closed. Nobody would touch a sexy Western. The cowboy kisses his horse, maybe, but that's all. So Draw Hudson looked like a dead duck, but I know Hollywood, so I kept at it. I kept at it, and every time a new Stewart novel was published, I started all over again. Do you know what all this cost me, Blake? Have you got any idea? This isn't half-ass New York stuff, you know, where you submit a manuscript and maybe exchange a few phone calls or buy a few drinks. This is Hollywood stuff, where you've got to sleep with some sonovabitch's wife, or escort his daughter around, or maybe sleep with him, too, if the wind blows that way. When I say I broke my back, I mean that, brother. I worked like hell."

"So?" I said.

"So. So nothing. So you two shrewd operators step in, and maybe you have an agreement, and maybe you haven't. But you're screwing up the plum pudding because I've finally got a guy ready to sign on the dotted line, with tons of money behind him, and all solid stuff. Becker has a list of credits as long as my arm. He produced for all the big studios, and now he's an independent who can get more money than God. He's anxious to do Draw Hudson. He's so anxious, he can't sleep nights. But you step in and louse up the china closet with your goddamned alleged agreement, and Becker gets the D.T.'s."

"He didn't seem too frightened a few minutes ago," I said.

"Is he here?" Rutherford asked.

"He's getting into something dry," I said.

Rutherford didn't question this. "If he's not scared now, it's because I'm a shrewd bastard, too, Blake. I didn't get into this business yesterday. I've been at it a long time now. I talked Becker blue in the face after I spoke to you yesterday. I told him if you had an agreement, you'd show it. I advised him to go ahead, and lawsuits be damned. That's the trouble, Blake. When two smart-angle boys are up against each other, it's every man for the rowboats, and the women and children be damned. This deal is going through. If you've got an agreement, let's see it. We're calling your bluff, and the ante's high."

"I've got an agreement," I said half-heartedly.

"Fine. You can bring it to the party."

"What party?"

"Tonight, Blake. Right here. In honor of the contract-signing."

"What?"

Rutherford nodded. "There'll be some real bigwigs, Blake. And the press, of course. We're going to get a million bucks worth of free publicity, and Becker'll announce that the first novel he'll film will be *Gunsmoke*. Come along—and bring your agreement."

"You're not behaving very shrewdly," I said.

"No?"

"No, Rutherford. I'll be here, all right, with the agreement, and maybe with my lawyer."

"Fine," Rutherford said. He extended his hand. "No hard feelings?"

"None whatever."

"I didn't think there would be. We understand each other."

Cam had been silent all this time, staring out at the pool, seemingly above all this bickering for her brainchild. She turned to me now, and her lashes were sooty, and the wind lifted her hair from her shoulders. She smiled me that lazy smile and said, "Do come, Josh. There'll be plenty to drink, and stuff."

"You couldn't keep me away," I said.

Cam smiled again, and this time Rutherford smiled with her.

8.

The drive back to the city was a pleasant one. With the top down and a fresh breeze lapping at my face, I was comfortably cool. I kept thinking about that party, though, and the god-damned missing agreements, and that spoiled the pleasantness for me. When I hit the city, the furnace consumed me. It was hotter than I'd ever known it to be. By the time I reached the office, I was dripping wet.

I walked into the reception room and nodded at Jeanette, who looked crisp and cool, thank the wonders of air conditioning.

"Oh hello, Mr. Blake," she said.

"Hiya. Tim in?"

"Yes, sir. He's marketing, I believe."

"Good."

I walked through the reception room and then I knocked on Tim's door.

"Come in," he called.

I went into his office, where he sat with his sleeves rolled up and his tie yanked down. A pile of manuscripts was on the desk in front of him, and I heard the hum of the air-conditioning unit. A smoldering cigarette was in a tray near his right elbow. He was studying a green card tacked to one of the manuscripts, and he looked up when I walked in, and then smiled.

"Man, you look beat," he said.

"That's not the word for it, Tim. How's it going?"

"Fairly smoothly."

"Any sales?"

"A rewrite request from Fawcett. That's it."

"Anything else of interest?"

"Some checks. I left those on your desk. Mostly sales we knew about. One surprise, though."

"Which?"

"A short short to Volitant."

"Oh, that's nice. Who?"

"O'Donnell."

"Fine. That should stop his screaming for an advance."

"Yeah. He's about due, isn't he?"

I nodded. "Look, Tim, I'll be locking in for a while. Tell Jeanette, will you? As far as anyone's concerned, I'm not here."

"Right."

"On second thought, I'll tell her myself. I want her to get someone for me."

"Okay."

"Keep at it, boy."

Tim nodded and turned back to his marketing, and I left him and went into my own office. I glanced at the checks he'd left on my desk, looked at a few memos he had put there, and then buzzed Jeanette.

"Sir?"

"Jeanette, would you get Roy Parsons for me, please? His number is in the book."

"Yes, sir. Sir?"

"What is it, Jeanette?"

"About Lydia…"

"Yes?"

"The police were here again this morning, asking all sorts of questions. It's a shame, isn't it, sir? I mean, she was such a lovely girl."

"Yes. Was Sergeant Di Luca here?"

"Yes."

"That figures. All right, hon, will you make that call, please? And after this, I'm not in to anyone, savvy?"

"Yes, sir."

I clicked off and studied the ceiling, leaning back in my chair. In a few minutes, Jeanette buzzed with my call, and I lifted the receiver.

"Hello."

"Hi, Josh. What goes?"

"Nothing much. How's your end?"

"Can't kick. You got troubles?"

"In a small way."

"Shoot. I'm ears."

"What do you know about David Becker?"

"Becker, Becker. Big man, Josh. Lots of hits, a few Academy Awards. Why?"

"What about his money?"

"What about it?"

"Has he got any? He's an independent now, you know."

"I know."

"So?"

"So what do you want to know, Josh?"

"I want to know if he's using his own dough on his latest venture, or if he's being backed."

"I can check. Is this that Cam Stewart deal?"

"Yes, but keep it under your lid."

"I'm a clam. I'll call you back, Josh."

"Right. Thanks a lot, Roy."

"Don't mention it."

He hung up, and I sat back and waited, and then realized it might take a little time. Roy was public relations man for one of the big movie-industry trade journals. If there was anyone who could find out anything about someone in the industry, he was the boy. I'd done favors for him in the past, and he owed me one—but he'd have helped even if he had no obligations. I got restless just then and decided I could use a walk to the john down the hall.

I felt in my pocket to be sure I had the key, walked around my desk and across the room, and then out into the reception room.

"I thought you were in," the voice said. I didn't recognize it, but I looked up quickly. At first, I didn't even recognize the voice's owner, but then it registered.

The same black hair that hung over his forehead, the same shaggy brows, the same pig-bristled jaw. My writer friend. The one I'd tossed out on his keister yesterday.

"What the hell do you want?" I asked.

"David Gunnison," he said. "You remember me?"

"I remember you," I told him. "I thought we'd concluded our business."

"You thought wrong."

"Look, Gunnison, why don't you get the hell out of here? This time I'll call the police, so help me."

Gunnison smiled. "I don't think you will, Blake."

There was something crafty in his eyes, something that made me stop short and take notice for a moment. He looked like a man holding four aces, and begging for the guy with the straight flush to bet into him. "What's on your mind?" I asked cautiously.

"My book."

"Again?"

"Yes. I think maybe you'd better take it on."

"Why? Give me a good reason why."

"I've got a good reason. I've got a reason that might interest you a lot. It might interest you a whole lot."

"Talk sense, Gunnison."

"Don't get smart, Blake. You're in no position to get smart."

I started to walk past him. "If you're going to talk gibberish get out of my way."

He laid a beefy hand on my chest and said, "Just a second, pal."

I brushed his hand aside and said, "Don't pal me, pal."

"You're going to take my book on, Blake. We're going to be author and agent, so you might just as well start changing your attitude now. Like I say, you're in no position..."

"Oh, get the hell..."

He shoved me again, and this time I got sore, and I shoved back, ramming my hand hard against his chest. Gunnison wheeled back a few paces and then ducked his head like a bull coming in for the kill. I stood my ground, and when he came I kept up the bull-fight pretense, stepping aside like a matador and planting the toe of my shoe against his wide buttocks. He sprawled forward on his face, and I thought, this is going to be another picnic. This is going to be another game of pick up Gunnison and throw him out into the hall.

Gunnison had other ideas. When I reached down for him, he rolled over and grabbed my wrist, pulling me forward and kicking me in the stomach at the same time. I went head over heels onto my back, and then Gunnison was up and reaching down for *me*.

I wasn't as quick as he had been. He got his big hands into my collar, and he pulled me toward his outstretched fist, and when it connected, I saw Saturn and a few of the other planets. Jeanette screamed and plugged in one of her wires, and I figured she was calling the police if she had sense enough to do that. I didn't do much more figuring then because Gunnison was bearing down on me, and there was a confident look in his eyes, and that goddamned smug, superior smirk on his face again—the smirk of the man with the four aces. He lashed out with his fist, catching me over the shoulder, spinning me half around. I started to turn, and his other fist caught me on the throat, almost choking me.

I brought up a sharp right uppercut in a reflexive movement, and it whistled by his head, just missing him. But he got cautious, and he began backing away, and by this time I was real mad, and if Gunnison were a smart man he'd have hopped the next plane to Outer Mongolia.

Gunnison wasn't a smart man. He must have seen the glint in my eyes, and the set of my lips, but he stood there smiling smugly, and I closed in.

I feinted at his belly, and he brought down his big, farmer hands and that was just what I wanted. I lashed out with a straight left that caught him right on the button. His head rocked back, and a wash of sweat shook loose from his mane of black hair. He shook his head, and blinked at my other hand coming toward his face.

I caught him on the nose, and I felt the bone crunch, and then blood was spilling out onto his lip, and a look of unbearable pain crossed his face. I threw one more at him, and he screamed, "You filthy bastard! I'll show you, you bastard! I'll show you!"

I didn't hear him. I kept hitting him until he was on the floor again, and then I picked him up and carried him to the door, and really threw him into the hall this time.

He lay on the hall floor, looking up at me, and I kept my fists clenched and I shouted, "Now get this straight, Gunnison. You come back here again, and you're through, finished. I'll break every bone in your goddamned body, and then I'll throw you out the window. Just remember that, you bastard. Just remember it and stay far away. Stay out of this building. Stay off Fifth Avenue, you bastard. In fact, get the hell out of the city, because I'll kill you no matter where the hell I see you again. You got that, Gunnison?"

"I'll be back," he said. He spoke around the handkerchief he held to his nose. The handkerchief was rapidly turning red, and he kept dabbing it at his nose and talking around it. "I'll be back, Blake, and you'll listen when you've cooled down. You'll listen, 'cause you're in no position…"

"Try it," I said. "If you like a broken face, try it. Just try it, Gunnison."

I slammed the door on his words and walked over to where Jeanette sat near the switchboard. Her face was white, and she had her knuckles pressed against her mouth.

"Did you call the police?" I asked.

"N…no, sir. D…do you want me to?"

"No, never mind. If you see that sonovabitch walk in here again, buzz me right away."

"Yes, sir." She stared at me with her eyes wide, her knuckles back against her mouth again.

"Did Roy Parsons call back?"

"Yes, sir." She was still staring at me.

"What the hell's wrong?" I snapped.

"Your…your face, sir. It's bleeding."

I felt my cheek, the same cheek that had been kicked open by the guy who'd cornholed me at Lydia's place. Gunnison had reopened the cut with his big fists. I swore and said, "Never mind that, I'll fix it. Get Parsons for me, will you?"

I went into my office, found some iodine and a band-aid, and covered the cut. My hands were still trembling, and inside me there was a hatred big enough to fill the Empire State Building. That sonova…

The buzzer sounded, and I clicked on, and Jeanette told me she had Roy. I lifted the phone.

"Hello, Roy."

"Hi, Josh. I've got the dope."

"Let's hear it."

"He's being backed."

"Good," I said. "How many people?"

"Two, from what I could get. You want their names?"

"Yes," I said. "Please."

"Andrew Jamison," Roy said, pausing for my appreciative whistle, "and Bertram Nester."

"You're sure about this, Roy? I'm going to move on it, and I don't want to screw myself."

"This is gospel, Josh."

"Okay, Roy. Thanks a million."

"Nada," Roy said. "That's Spanish for…"

"I know."

"Okay, boy, good luck."

"Thanks."

"So long."

Roy hung up, and I smiled at the receiver, and then placed it back in the cradle. Becker was being financed, and the financiers were as big as you could want them. That meant Becker could be scared. And if Rutherford was being shrewd, as he'd kept telling me, this was one baby who could be just as goddamned shrewd.

I thought of Cam Stewart.

And I wondered what would have happened if we'd taken that little swim, if Rutherford hadn't popped in when he had. I shrugged the thought aside, dialed Celebrity Service and found out where David Becker was staying, telling them to bill me for the information. There was a chance he'd be back from Cam's place by now. And if not, I'd wait. I'd wait a long time.

✿

It occurred to me on the way over to Becker's hotel that I'd almost forgotten my murdered partner. Becker's place was a few blocks from the office, so I was walking it, and when the thought came, it gave me something of a jolt. I wondered what the case would be if the situation had been reversed. Suppose it had been Del who'd found *me* dead on my office floor? If I knew Del, he'd probably have arranged for a big publicity tie-in, hoping to get every mystery writer in the field. Well, I wasn't a hell of a lot more merciful. The guy had been murdered, and his mistress after him, and all I worried about was a pending movie deal.

Except the two were tied together. I felt I knew Di Luca didn't share my views, and I knew that a lot of unrelated things can happen, sometimes confusing the true picture, but I still felt the movie deal was connected with the two murders. And by shoving at the deal, by watching the people most interested in the deal, I felt certain I'd get to the bottom of the deaths.

Don't misunderstand me. I wasn't playing cop. I'd never played cop in my life, and I certainly wasn't starting now. I was, I suppose, primarily interested in the deal, and what the murders could do to kill the deal. But at the same time, I didn't like the idea of someone going around taking pot-shots at the agency personnel. When someone gets a wanton gun, you never know who's going to be next.

Which was a selfish outlook, too, I suppose.

All right then, the whole damned setup was selfish. So be proud of yourself, you bastard. You want a Caddy, and not a Buick. You want a sprawling house with a swimming pool, and not an apartment with an electric fan. You want three-hundred-dollar suits. You want money. That makes you a bastard.

Bastard or no, Del is dead. Lydia is dead, too, and you can't help the dead by shedding a lot of tears. The police were on it, and the police would probably solve it if they took Di Luca off the case, which they probably would not do, and so the whole thing would be dumped into the open file and the hell with it.

How many perfect murders are committed every year, anyway? How many every day?

I couldn't guess.

I couldn't guess, and I didn't want to guess, because there was still a big feeling of guilt inside me, as if I should have been more actively concerned with finding the murderer, and the movie deal be damned.

But the movie deal was big, and I wasn't going to dump it. No. Let the police find the murderer. That was their job.

Sure, I told myself. Sure.

But I didn't believe it for a minute.

I got Becker's room number from the desk clerk and then took the elevator up.

I wasn't prepared for the blonde who answered the door. She wore a cocoa-brown sweater that was simply crazy in this heat, but she didn't seem to mind very much. If anything, she seemed to thrive in it. She seemed to thrive everywhere, in fact, from the unhidden curve of her breast, to the flowing curve of her hip, to her legs, to her throat, to everywhere. She was one of the most thriving creatures I had ever seen.

She smiled now and said, "Yes?"

"Mr. Becker, please," I said.

"Who's calling?"

"May I come in? I'm not selling anything, really." I smiled, and she smiled back, and then she opened the door and I walked into the suite. It was a nice layout, and it was probably costing Becker a pretty penny. I looked at the girl again. She reminded me of someone. She was very tall, and her blonde hair was cropped close to her head. She had bright blue eyes that fairly sparkled, and she wore a pale orange lipstick, and that damned cocoa-brown sweater that made it difficult to remember anything else.

"You look familiar," I said.

"I'm not," she answered, smiling. "Nor do I intend to be."

"No, really. Haven't we…met?" I asked lamely.

"Oh, brother."

"Corny, I know. I'm serious, though. You remind me of someone I…"

I remembered then. The blonde in the half-slip and bra. The one I'd found at my kitchen table, puffing on a cigarette. I stared at her hard. No, it wasn't she, but it could have passed for her in a crowd.

"No," I said. "Sorry. I was mistaken."

"I still don't know who you are."

"A friend of Dave's," I lied.

"Who?"

"A friend. I want to surprise him."

"If you're a friend of Dave's, you know he doesn't go in for surprises."

"Where is he?" I asked.

She gestured with her head toward a closed door. "In there. With his lawyers. Working on a contract."

"Oh. Who are you?"

"His secretary."

"Traveling?"

"Sure." She saw the look that flitted over my face and hastily added, "Don't get ideas, Buster."

I shrugged. "How long will Dave be?"

She shrugged, too, and she did it much better than I. "An hour, two. Who knows?"

"That's what I figured," I said. I started for the closed door.

"Hey!" the blonde shouted. "Where are you going?"

"To surprise Dave."

"But…"

I already had my hand on the doorknob. I twisted it, and the blonde started running across the room, but I was inside, and I slammed the door behind me and looked into the startled faces.

Becker's face was in the middle, round as a cue ball. On either side, like cue sticks with chalked tips, were two long-faced lawyers.

Becker stood up quickly and said, "What are you doing here, you chiseler?"

"I bring sad tidings, Caesar," I said.

Becker turned to one of the lawyers. "What the hell is this madman talking about?"

"Lend me your ears, friends," I said.

"Look, Blake…"

"I know, Becker. You're busy. You've got to get this contract all worked out before the big shindig tonight. Cam'll sign on the dotted line then, and everybody will break a magnum of champagne on her luscious head." I shook my own, not-so-luscious head. "No dice, Becker."

"Your agreement again, huh, crook?" He looked around him hastily, to see if there were any swimming pools in the vicinity.

"Yes, my friend, my agreement. I'm going to be at the party."

"So come. So who cares?"

"The angels, Becker."

"What?"

"The backers, Becker, the backers."

"What?" he spluttered, still not grasping it.

"Becker's backers. Andrew Jamison and Bertram Nester. And I'm going to tell them you don't own TV or radio rights. I'm going

to shout it to the goddamned rooftops, and they're both going to
turn green, Becker. They're going to vomit and they're going to run
like hell because no one's going to invest with a lawsuit swinging
over his head." I paused. "Get the idea, Becker?"

"You…you…"

"I would, Becker. I would, and I will, and I'm going to. I'll be
there with bells on, and we'll see how many people will be
willing to invest in this turkey once they find out what the score
is. You can't go around me, Becker, so you might as well come
to me."

"You…you…"

"Yes, me, me. I'm the guy. Papa Blake. It all has to come
through me, or the deal gets it in the ass. If you want that, fine.
But don't say I didn't warn you." I started for the door, feeling
damned good. "I'll see you at the party, Becker."

I swung out and slammed the door behind me, almost knocking
over the blonde. I reached down and patted her on the fanny, and
she looked up, surprised as hell.

I went to the garage, got the Buick, and drove straight for Gail
Gilbert's place in Yonkers. With Del dead, she was, after all,
almost a partner, and I thought I should keep her informed on
the latest developments. Besides, I was more than a little worried about her. She hadn't been home earlier, and with some
damned idiot running around with a .45 in his mitt, there was
no telling what could happen. I pulled up in front of the house,
saw that the white bamboo drapes were drawn back, and sighed
in relief.

I pressed the panel in the door jamb, heard the buzzer go off
inside, and then waited. I didn't hear any footsteps, so I was
surprised when the door opened.

"Josh!" Gail said. "What a surprise!"

"Hi," I said.

I followed her into the spacious living room, tastefully furnished in whites and blacks and greys. The interior here reminded me of the approach to Gunsmoke Acres, except that this was severely modern, with the cold, sterile look broken only by some bright orange throw-pillows on the long couch. Gail, in keeping with the room, was wearing black pedal-pushers, and a white, long-sleeved blouse. The blouse was buttoned to the third button from the throat, and that left a lot of unbuttoned area. She'd apparently been out in the sun, and it had brought out a dusting of freckles on her nose, and had put a high flush into her cheeks.

"Sit down," she said. "Can I get you something to drink?"

"All right."

"What'll it be?"

"Gin and bitters should be nice."

"Sorry, no gin."

"What have you got?"

"There's a batch of whiskey sours I mixed. Could you go for one of those?"

"Fine."

"Be with you in a minute." She walked into the kitchen and I heard her rummaging around in the refrigerator. I heard her cracking ice, and I called, "Hey, I thought they were already mixed."

"I'm just freshening them."

"Okay."

I heard the sound of ice dumped into a shaker, and then the shaker being pounded for all it was worth.

She stopped shaking and called, "What did you think of Di Luca?"

"Barging in yesterday, you mean?"

"Yes." She was shaking again.

"That was my idea, Gail, I sent him when I thought you were in trouble."

"He told me he made it all the way up here in ten minutes. Do you believe that?"

"With sirens blasting, why not?"

"I thought he was nice. Sort of cute."

"If you go for spooks."

"I also think he's a good cop." She was back in the living room now, with the cocktail shaker in one hand, and two whiskey-sour glasses in the other. She put the glasses down on the coffee table in front of the couch, and then poured both glasses to the brim. Then she took the shaker out again.

"Whiskey sours should have cherries and orange peels," she said, when she came back.

"We can forego both," I told her. I lifted the glass and waited. "Here's to finding Del's murderer."

"And Lydia's," she added.

"And Lydia's." We touched glasses and took a sip. Gail mixed one hell of a strong sour.

"And here's to the movie deal," I said.

"Here's to it." We drank again. "Does it look good?" she asked.

"Very good. They don't know which way to turn now, Gail. I'm sure they'll come across."

"Good." She drank more of her sour and then said, "Do you think there's a tie-in? Between the movie deal and the murders, I mean?"

"Yes."

"I thought so, too. Apparently, Di Luca doesn't."

"No, I know that."

"He's a frank man, isn't he?"

"How so?"

"He asked me if I knew Del was shacking with Lydia. That's just the way he put it."

"What'd you tell him?"

"I said I didn't know anything about it."

"Why?"

"I don't want to get involved in this, Josh. It's bad enough that I hated the bastard. With a cop like Di Luca sniffing around, anything might happen. I'll be damned if I'm going to wind up paying for a double murder."

"Di Luca will probably find out, anyway."

"Well, if he does, I'll lie again. Truthfully, I don't give a damn if the murderer never gets caught—so long as my hands are clean."

"Well…"

"You think I'm a bitch, don't you? You think I should go around weeping all over the place, pretending I'm sorry. Well, I'm not sorry. I'm glad he got it, and I'm glad he's dead." She looked at me significantly. "And I'm glad I'm free now."

"Gail, the guy was killed only yesterday. I don't care how you felt about him, but…"

"I'm cold-hearted, is that what you think? You think I'm cold right down to my toes. No, Josh. I'm just godawful glad, that's all. Glad to be rid of him. He was a lying, conniving, thieving cheat. I'm glad he's dead."

I stood up and walked across the room, wondering what I could say to that. I supposed she had reason enough to be delighted, but it still seemed strange to hear someone talk like that. There was something almost abnormal about it. Like…like dancing on a coffin.

I heard Gail put her glass down on the coffee table, and then she padded across the room silently, barefoot, and stood behind me.

"Josh," she said softly.

I turned, saw the look in her eyes, and quickly put my glass to my mouth. I drained the sour and then asked, "Any more of these?"

Gail eyed me curiously. "In the kitchen."

I picked up her empty glass on the way, walked into the kitchen, and found the shaker on the top shelf of the refrigerator. I took it out, closed the door, gave it a few hearty shakes, and then filled both glasses. I was heading back to the living room when Gail came into the kitchen after me.

I handed her the sour, and she leaned back against the door jamb, blocking the exit.

She sipped a little of her drink, looked at me over the edge of the glass, and said, "What are you afraid of, Josh?"

"Me? Nothing."

She smiled. "Oh, but you are."

"Honey…"

"Don't use words like that. Honey, or darling, or anything like that. I don't want to hear them."

"Look, hon…"

"Don't, I said!" She threw off the drink in one hasty gulp, and then slammed it down on the sink top, almost breaking the glass.

"All right, Gail, what *do* you want?"

"You know what I want. You know damn well what I want!"

"This is very flattering, Gail, but…"

"Oh, shut your goddamned mouth!"

"Gail…"

"You think it has to be you, you egotistical ape?" She seemed about to say more. Then she changed her mind, shook her head, and snapped, "Oh, get the hell out of here. Run along. Go play agency."

"Sure," I said. I put down my drink and started through the door. Gail sucked in her stomach to let me by, and then as I passed her, she threw her arms around my neck.

"Take this with you," she said almost viciously.

She rammed her mouth against mine, brought her whole

body close. Her mouth moved furiously, and her tongue pushed against my closed lips.

I shoved her away. "Gail, for Christ's sake!"

Her eyes sparked, and her chest heaved.

Del was dead, and I was romping around with a movie deal. And Gail was behaving like a mare in heat, only I wasn't having any, thanks.

She backed out of the doorway, her hands tight, her eyes still flashing. There was hatred in those eyes.

"He's dead," I said lamely. "He's only just…"

"You are, too," she shouted. "Get the hell out of here! Get out before…"

"Gail, be sensible. I'm only…"

"Get out!" she screamed. "Get out! Get out, get out!"

I left.

9.

A mild breeze blew in over the river that night. It swept over from LaGuardia Airport, swerved past Riker's Island, smacked North Brother Island, and then swung downtown past Hell Gate and the Triboro Bridge, followed the river, and then rustled through the young trees lining the East River Drive.

When it poured through my open window, it was still fresh. It blew the curtains high, and I smiled and sighed heavily. It was a rain wind, and the city needed rain. The city needed a lot of rain to wash the heat out of the pavements. And the blood.

There had been a lot of blood, so far. Too much.

I sniffed of the mild breeze, and I listened to the curtains flapping against the wall, and I dressed very carefully.

I didn't know whether or not the party was going to be a formal one. I wasn't taking any chances, though. The press would be there, and if I intended setting them on their ears, a tux was as good a costume for the occasion as any—especially if everyone else wore one.

I'd shaved close, showered, put on a fresh set of underwear, and was pulling on my trousers now, standing in my black-stockinged feet. I zipped up the fly, buttoned the top button, and then slipped the suspenders over my shoulders. I noticed I didn't have a shirt on, dropped the suspenders, slipped into the shirt and then adjusted the suspenders again. The breeze was still cool, but it was more hurried now, and I knew it would rain soon.

I pulled on my shoes and laced them, and then went to the dresser for my cuff links and studs. I found the studs, but no cuff links. I shrugged, tied my black tie, and then walked to the back of the apartment. The living room and kitchen ran the length of the rear wall, their windows opening on the low apartment building across the areaway. I rummaged around in the cigarette boxes in the living room, I'd left cuff links in strange places in my day. They were nowhere to be found. I swore a little, mildly, because the breeze was such a relief, and started looking in earnest. I went through the drop-leaf desk in the living room. No cuff links. I went through the bar, searching in the shot glasses. No cuff links.

I walked into the kitchen and started nosing around there. I looked in the sugar bowl, and in the toaster, and in the silverware drawer, I was beginning to feel a little warm, and then I realized the kitchen window was closed, and I fairly blew my lid.

I walked to the window with my shirt sleeves flapping, and threw open the blind. I reached for the window, ready to snap it open.

The shots came then.

Two in a row, fast, so fast that they sounded almost like a single explosion. Like backfire in the street below.

Except that the window shattered into a thousand flying fragments. I dropped instantly, below the sill, hugging the floor, waiting for more shooting.

I waited for ten minutes, but nothing more came. I lifted my head cautiously then, and peered over the edge of the sill. The roof of the building across the areaway was almost level with my window. It didn't take much deep contemplation to figure where the shots had come from.

There was no one on the roof now.

I looked down into the areaway at the lighted windows of the building opposite. Not one head was looking out of any window. A backfire, they'd probably figured.

I swallowed hard and turned away from the window. My hands were trembling as I got the foxtail and dustpan from the broom closet. I began sweeping up the shards of glass, and my hands kept trembling.

I swept up all the glass, deposited it in the step-on can, and then walked back to the window. The roof opposite was almost level, but not quite. It was a little higher than, my window, which meant the marksman had shot down at me. I backed away from the window, remembering the way the glass had suddenly shattered.

I moved to the far wall of the room, searched the wall near the floorboard, and found the two slugs imbedded in the plaster where they'd knocked big chunks out of the wall.

A .45?

Maybe. My hands started shaking again, and the rain came at that moment.

It swept from the sky like an avenger, lashing the roof opposite. It was a noisy rain, like a wave lashing a beach. It came hard, and it came steadily, and I ran around the apartment closing windows. When I reached the smashed kitchen window, I drew the blind tight, and hoped the floor wouldn't get too wet.

Lightning flashed in the sky, and the belated bellow of thunder rocked the house. It was a wonderful evening for a party, all right.

I wiped my face, and started searching for my cuff links again. I finally found them in a small cup without a handle. The cup contained two wrapped toothpicks, some ticket stubs, and the cuff links.

Why me? I thought abruptly.

Why the hell me?

Stupid, I told myself. You're the guy who's going to upset the applecart. You're the guy who's going to that party, and you're going to scare off Becker's backers. That's why you. You've been elected target of the year. The only other people who knew anything about the Cam Stewart deal have already been killed, and you can't kill the dead. There's only one other joker who knows about that agreement, and that, my friend, is you. Y-O-U.

Simple motives, Di Luca had said. Well, there is something sinisterly simple about a goddamned slug from a .45. Very simple, pal. It leaves a big hole, and big things are simple. It also leaves a clean hole.

And it also leaves you dead, and that's the ultimate in simplicity.

Can it, I told myself. I finished dressing, and then I went down for the car.

It was still raining. I hadn't minded it when I thought it would be a short summer storm. It was more than that now. It was something fierce. I backed the car out of the garage, and the rain lashed at the windshield. I had the wipers going full blast, but it was hell seeing, and I drove slowly and began thinking about the party and hoping I wouldn't be too late. It would be a hell of a thing to get there after the announcement had been made. I wanted to be there before the press got the story. I wanted to squelch it before it was released, so the backers would back off, leaving Becker with an empty sack.

But I drove slowly. If someone at the party had taken a shot at me, or hired someone to shoot at me, maybe they thought the bullets had scored. In which case, they were in no hurry. The party would proceed along normal channels, building to a nice climax, at which point Cam would affix her signature to the contracts, the band would play a neat flourish, and the reporters' pencils would begin scribbling. Besides, the road was slippery and wet, and whether you're killed by a .45 or another car, the difference is the same. I didn't feel like spending the night with Saint Peter.

There was very little traffic heading for Connecticut, and the road was as black as a witch's heart. Most of the traffic was headed for New York, which made matters dandy. I kept squinting against the bright lights that flashed across the rain-soaked windshield. It was ginger-peachy driving, pleasant on the nerves. There was just a long tunnel of blackness, and then *wham!* a pair of lights stabbing out of that tunnel, blinding the hell out of you.

I kept driving slowly, turning my eyes to the white curbing on the road whenever one of the bright-lights maniacs sped past. I didn't notice the lights behind me for quite some time, and even when I did notice them, I figured them for just another car and that was all.

But I was traveling at a snail's pace, and the city-bound traffic was really moving at a fast clip. There are guys who'll burn up the road, even when it's wet, but a skid is one thing I really fear. Any other kind of trouble, you can work your way out of—except no brakes, of course. A skid is just the same as no brakes, only worse. It's the one time you completely lose control of the car. You tug at the wheel, and you try to follow all the directions you had about turning your nose into the skid, but you can't get away from the fact that the car isn't yours anymore. There's someone else at the wheel, and he's got a skull-bare head, and he's grinning evilly, and if he wants the car, he'll take it. You haven't anything to say about it once the skid grabs you. He's at the wheel, and it's his car, and you just sit back and grit your teeth and wait.

That's why I drove slowly, and I was surprised to see the lights behind me creeping along at the same pace.

I mentally tagged the driver as another careful Joe, not paying him a hell of a lot of mind. The traffic heading for New York began to thin out, leaving just the black tunnel with my own lights pushing through it. And, of course, the car behind me.

I kept my eyes on the road, mostly. But occasionally, I glanced into the rear-view mirror and saw the lights of the other car. I guess they were comforting, in a way. When you're driving on a black road, you feel as though you're on the edge of the universe, and that you may pitch off into nothingness within the next few feet.

I turned on the radio, trying to get some music. I got a lot of static instead. I cursed the lightning, snapped off the radio, and continued driving slowly.

The car behind me, matching my speed, kept a good thirty feet between us. And then the lights swung out, and I realized the guy was tired of the pace and was ready to pass me. I hugged the side of the road as the car pulled alongside. He kept abreast of me for a few moments, and then stepped on the gas. I still didn't look to my left. When a guy is passing, he's passing. What the hell, it's a simple maneuver.

But this guy made it difficult.

He passed and then cut over sharply, bringing his car directly in front of my own.

I shouted, "Hey!" to no one, and then jammed on the brakes. The big Buick's tires tried to grip the road, but it was too slippery. They held for an instant, and then the rear end shrieked and went into the skid, and the skull-faced character took the wheel while I waited. The car swung around, and I gritted my teeth and held the wheel tight. It stopped about an inch short of the other car, and I sighed in relief until I saw both doors of the other car snap open.

It came fast and clear then. It hadn't been an accident. The guy had deliberately cut me short, had intentionally caused me to stop. There were two of them, and they came toward the car quickly, I figured my chances rapidly. My car was twisted at a curious angle that made backing off an impossibility. I couldn't go forward because their car was blocking the road.

I had no choice. I locked the doors and waited, watching the two men advance through the driving rain.

One came around to the driver's seat and tried the door there. When he found it was locked, he reached in under his coat, wasting no time. I saw the glint of a gun in his hand, and I ducked because I expected him to fire. Instead, he swung the gun butt-up, smashed it against the window, and then stuck his hand inside, opening the door.

"Out," he said.

"What is this?"

"Out. Come on."

"Look…"

"Jesus, Mac, it's raining. Let's move."

I looked at the gun in his hand, and the bore seemed like an unusually big one. I pulled up the collar of my trench coat and stepped out of the car. The rain soaked me the instant I hit the road.

"What is this?" I asked again.

"This guy must like the rain, Charlie," the first man said. "Come on, we'll talk in the car."

They led me to their car, a new Olds, and I squeezed into the front seat between them.

The one called Charlie stepped on the gas, and I turned my head and said, "Hey, what about my car?"

"You can pick it up in the morning," Charlie said. "It'll be okay."

"Listen…"

"It'll be okay," Charlie repeated. "Radio says the rain'll stop soon."

"The window…" I started.

"I'm sorry about the window," the first guy said.

"You shouldn't have broken the window, Ed," Charlie told him.

"Yeah," Ed said sorrowfully. "I'm sorry, believe me."

I sighed and looked back at the car. Charlie had left the parking lights on, to avoid any collision, I supposed. Still, the battery…

"This is one hell of a thing," I said. "What the hell is going on?"

"It's a bitch, I know," Ed said cheerfully. "Well, what the hell are you going to do? That's life."

"Suppose you let me in on it," I said bitterly.

"Sure," Ed said, still cheerfully. "We're having a party."

"I wasn't invited," I said.

"You are now. We're inviting you. Personally."

"Sorry," I said. "I've got a previous engagement."

"We know. That's why we're having this party."

"Oh, I get it," I said.

"Good," Charlie answered. "It's a pleasure to deal with someone who's intelligent." He kept his foot pressed to the accelerator. He wasn't driving fast. He kept the car at a steady 50 mph, but on a slippery road, that was too fast for me.

"Another beating, huh?" I asked. "Another football match. You bat me around a little, and then drop me in a ditch. Fine."

"What gave you that idea?" Ed asked, surprised.

"Don't try to snow me, friend. I've been through the mill already. Who gave you the idea? That's what I'd like to know."

"That's a secret," Charlie said. He smiled in the light of the dashboard, and I looked at the silhouette of his profile. "But there's no beating attached. Relax."

"This is a party," Ed added. "Didn't you understand?"

"Who are the guests?"

"You."

"And the host?"

"We're the hosts. Me and Charlie. It'll be a nice party, don't worry. No rough stuff, believe me."

"Why?"

"Why what?"

"Why the kidnap? That's a federal offense, you know."

"Kidnap? Who said anything about a kidnap? Was someone kidnaped? Hell, Mac, this is just a party. You'll see."

"Sure. Why?"

"Because you don't want to go to that other shindig. It'll be dull."

Very dull, I thought. Just a little contract-signing, that's all. Just several thousand dollars riding on it, that's all. Very dull. The thought was not an entertaining one. I lapsed into a sullen silence.

Charlie kept driving, and Ed lighted a cigarette, offering me one. I refused with a curt shake of my head. Ed put his package away, and smoked leisurely and contentedly.

Becker, Rutherford, or Stewart.

This crazy stunt had been hatched in one of their lucid minds. Crazy was the only word for it. It smacked of insanity—sheer, babbling, incoherent insanity. Did they really think this would make any difference? All right, so they'd go ahead and sign without me, but didn't they *know* I controlled the rights? Didn't they know I'd sue the pants off them? It was nuts, all right, and I couldn't understand it.

I couldn't understand a lot of things. And if this stunt was nuts, how about trying on the death of two people for size? How did that stack up in the Hall of Blame? If It was insane to kidnap a guy, how much crazier was it to kill someone?

I kept my silence. I still wasn't convinced that the boys weren't measuring me for a coffin. I kept my silence as the car nosed its way through the rain.

"Here we are," Charlie said, swinging the car onto a dirt road. "Right up ahead."

I looked through the windshield. The rain had slowed down,

and I saw a brightly lighted house up ahead. The boys were certainly not being cautious about this, and I began to breathe a little easier. Maybe there wasn't a bullet or a beating in the offing. With all those lights, maybe this *was* just a delaying action. The boys probably figured on sticking to their "just-a-little-party" story if they were caught. Just a little party. Yeah.

They both got out of the car as soon as Charlie had parked it, and I followed them reluctantly. Ed fell in behind me as Charlie unlocked the door to the house. The rain was coming down half-heartedly now, and I knew the storm would soon be over.

"That's a nice coat," Ed said.

"Thanks."

"Very nice."

"Thanks."

Charlie opened the door, and we all went into a spacious foyer.

"Ah," he said. "Feels good to be inside again. Take off your coat, Blake."

I took off my coat, and Charlie opened a hall closet, put it on a hanger, and then did the same for Ed's and his own coat. Ed locked the door, and we all went into the living room, and I had my first good look at them.

Ed was short, but built like a bull. He had close-cropped hair, and a massive jaw. He had a pudgy little nose and thin eyebrows. His eyes were blue and almost guileless. He looked like a butcher in the A & P.

Charlie was an affable-looking guy, too. He blinked whenever he spoke, and he squinted through thick glasses that covered his brown eyes. His teeth were bad, but there was a smile on his mouth. He had a long crooked nose that he rubbed occasionally with the back of his hand. He looked like a stockroom boy in the A & P.

"Well," I said. "Here we are."

"Sit down," Ed said genially. He waddled across the room on

his short legs, stopping alongside the liquor cabinet. "What'll you drink, Blake?"

"What've you got?"

"Anything."

"Vodka," I said, just to be mean.

Charlie laughed and rubbed his hook nose. "He thinks we're kidding, Ed. We've really got everything, Blake. You'll see."

Ed nodded and pulled a bottle with a multi-colored label from the cabinet. He fished out a sparkling glass, filled it to the brim, and brought it over to me.

"Vodka," he said. He sniffed at it, handed it to me, and added, "I think I'll try some of that. You, Charlie?"

"Okay. It can't kill me."

That reminded me of something. "You the boys who took some shots at me earlier tonight?"

Charlie looked up, surprised. Ed turned from the liquor cabinet, a hurt expression on his face. "Us?"

"Yes, you."

"Gee, Blake. I'm sorry you think that. I really am sorry."

"Yeah."

"Yeah."

"It wasn't us," he said, seriously concerned. "Someone shoot at you?"

"Never mind," I said.

"That's a shame," Charlie said, shaking his head. "Where's that vodka, Ed?"

Ed brought him the drink, and we all clinked glasses and then drank.

"Ah," Charlie said. "That was good."

Ed smacked his lips. "Powerful, though."

"Good and powerful. I'll have another." He handed his glass back to Ed. "How about you, Blake?"

"I like it slow," I said.

"Okay. You like poker, Blake?"

"Yes."

"Want to play a little? While the time away."

"Listen, are you guys serious?" I asked.

"About what?"

"Do you really intend keeping me here all night?"

Ed looked hurt again. He poured two more glasses of vodka and said nothing.

"Yes, we do," Charlie said, a surprised tone in his voice.

"Just keep me here?"

"That's all." Charlie leaned forward eagerly. "No hard feelings, Blake, honest. Why don't you just relax? Hell, we can have a good time here. You won't even miss the other party."

I sighed heavily. "Okay, break out the cards."

Ed smiled from ear to ear. "That's the spirit. By God, that's the spirit!" He brought the vodka to Charlie, and they drank together, and then Charlie went for the deck of cards. I sat on the couch and waited, finally knocking off the vodka. Charlie had been right. It was good—and powerful.

"A new deck," Charlie said, splitting the seal on a fresh pack. "So you know this is on the level."

I looked at the cards dubiously, but I didn't voice a comment. Ed shoved a chair close to the couch, and then moved a table over. The table pinned me effectively, and I admired the graciousness with which Ed had accomplished this simple maneuver. He was indeed a most genial host. He brought over the half-full bottle of vodka, together with a bottle that was still sealed. "Fresh supply," he said, beaming. He went into the kitchen then, while Charlie stayed with me, his gun in his shoulder holster. The gun was a .38, I noticed. When Ed came back, he was carrying a bowl of peanuts and a box of potato chips. "Food," he said, grinning.

He put these on the table alongside the vodka bottles, and

then pulled his chair up. Charlie sat down and began shuffling the cards.

"Dealer's choice?" he asked.

"Fine," Ed said, nodding his stubbled head. "Fine."

"A penny and two," Charlie said. "No two-cents bet unless a pair is showing, okay?" He nodded in agreement with himself. "No check-raising, okay? In a wild-card game, only a legitimate poker hand counts. No calling five aces or anything like that, okay?"

"Okay," Ed said.

"Okay," I said.

"More vodka?" Ed asked.

"Okay." I extended my glass, and Ed poured, and Charlie began dealing after I declined to cut.

We played a few rounds of straight draw poker, and I copped three hands in a row with two pair, a flush, and three jacks.

"We'd better watch this guy," Charlie said, reaching for the vodka bottle and pouring himself another drink. I was still on my second one, and keenly aware of the fact that this stuff was potent.

"He's a regular shark," Ed said. He picked up the cards, re-membered it was Charlie's deal, and handed the deck to him. "What'll it be, Charlie?"

"Seven-card stud. Here we go."

Charlie shuffled, shoved the deck to me for a cut, and I sliced it close to the top. He put the deck together again, and dealt two hole cards rapidly. Then he began dealing the face cards.

At the end of the third round, I had three kings showing, and both Charlie and Ed dropped out.

Ed took the cards and said, "Now we'll play some baseball."

"Some what?"

"Baseball."

"In here?" I said. "The room's a little small, isn't it?"

Ed laughed heartily and poured himself another shot of vodka. "It's a poker game," he said. "I'll explain it."

"Go ahead," Charlie said. He downed his glass and poured another. I sipped at mine and stuffed my mouth full of peanuts.

"You're not drinking at all," Ed said, a scold in his voice. "Come on, now. Don't be a party pooper."

I downed the vodka, felt it burn a hole clear to my stomach, and watched while Ed poured another glass.

"That's better," he said. "No sense spoiling the evening." I could have told him the evening had been spoiled already. Instead, I listened patiently while he explained baseball.

"It's just like seven-card stud," he said. "You get two down cards, and the rest up. You're allowed to use your best five cards for a poker hand."

"Okay," Charlie said. "That sounds fair." He lifted his glass and poured the contents down his throat. "Phew," he said.

"Where does the baseball come in?" I asked.

Ed grinned amiably. "Here's the difference," he said. "Nines and threes are wild. So you can use those for whatever you want."

"This commences to be a bastard game," Charlie said.

"No, it's good, it's good," Ed insisted. "Nines and threes are wild. However…"

"Here it comes," Charlie said. "A bastard game."

"…however, if you get a three, you have to match the pot."

"What do you mean, match the pot?" I asked. I drank a little of the vodka, and Charlie made a bottoms-up motion with his hand. I drained the glass.

"Match the pot," Ed said. "That means if there's twenty cents in the pot when you get a three, you put in twenty cents."

"A bastard game," Charlie said. He lifted his eyeglasses, wiped his eyes with forefinger and thumb, and then put the glasses back on his nose again. Then, with no loss of motion, he reached for the vodka bottle.

"Now, you got that?" Ed asked. "A three matches the pot. A nine doesn't match anything. But nines and threes are wild."

"I got it," I said. Charlie filled my glass, too.

"Now, when you get a four…"

"Fours are wild, too?" I asked.

"No."

"What then?" Charlie wanted to know. "You sure this is baseball? It sounds like Chinese checkers."

"This is baseball. When you get a four, that means you get an extra card."

"A what?"

"An extra card. At the end of the round, the dealer gives a down card to anyone who got a four."

"Jesus."

"Suppose I got a four in the hole? Do I get an extra card then?"

"No. It has to be showing."

"That's not fair," Charlie said. "Suppose I got a three in the hole? Do I have to match the pot?"

"No. Only if it's showing."

"All right," I said, "let's play a few hands. Where's the vodka?" I drained my glass and extended it, and Charlie reached out with two bottles, it seemed, to fill the glass.

We played two rounds of baseball, and we all had the knack of it by that time. Ed broke the seal on the second bottle of vodka, and we began working on that one. I thought of the Connecticut party, but I was beginning to have fun here, and I really couldn't remember very well why I wanted to go to that other party in the first place.

"Pass the vodka," Charlie said heavily.

I passed the vodka, and then I said, "Deal."

Charlie filled his glass. "Le's try another round of baseball, okay?"

"Okay," I said.

"Okay," Ed said. "Hey, do we need more p'tato ships?"

"No."

"No."

"Okay, deal."

"Ante, first."

We all anted two cents, and Charlie started dealing, giving us our two down cards. He gave Ed his face card then, and it was a three.

"Whoo," Charlie said. "You got to match the pot."

"S'nothing," Ed said, waving his hand grandly. "Hardly nothin' in there. Hardly nothin' at all. How mush is in there, Blake?"

I looked at the pennies on the table, knowing full well we'd each anted two cents, and that should have made a total of six cents.

"Jus' a minute," I said. I leaned over close to the table, and began counting the pennies. There were a lot of them. They were all over the table. "This's gonna break you, Ed," I said. "Y'better drop out."

Ed sat upright, dignity in every line of his face. "I c'n match it," he said. "How mush's in there?"

"Forty-seven cents," I said.

"Fifty-two cens," Charlie corrected.

"Jus' a minute, jus' a minute," Ed said. He poured another glass of vodka, downed it, and then counted the pennies we had anted. "I get forry-eight," he said.

"Le's split the difference."

"Okay. Between forry-eight and fifty-two."

"That's eight cens," Charlie said.

"An' split that, makes it four cents," I said, nodding my head vigorously. "Where's the vodka?"

"Right here," Charlie said. He filled my glass and I thanked him profusely and then swallowed its contents.

"So, add four cents to forry-eight, that comes to fifty-two."

"Sure, that's what I said," Charlie said.

"Sure," Ed agreed. He put a fifty-cent piece and two pennies in the center of the table.

"Big pot this trip," Charlie said.

"Yeah. Deal."

Charlie gave me my card. Another three.

"I'll be damned," Charlie said. "Another three. How do you like that? Say, this deck must be jinxed. Say, how you like that? Two threes in a row. Say, how's that?"

"Stinks," I said. "Where's the vodka?"

"Le's all have another li'l drink," Ed said. We filled all the glasses, clinked them together, and drank.

"Now," I said. "I gotta match the pot."

"Tha's easy," Ed said. "Jus' twice fifty-two."

"How much is that?" Charlie asked.

"Lemme figure it," I said. "I'm a l'rary agent, I figure p'centages all day long. Le'see now."

"Two times fifty-two. Tha's a hard one."

"No, s'easy. Le'see."

"Put in three dollars," Ed said. "Call it square."

"Sure," Charlie said. "We'll give you a break."

"Thanks, fellas," I said. "Thanks a lot."

"Don' mention it."

"Not at all."

I put in the three bucks, and Charlie dealt himself a card. A nine.

"Match the pot!" Ed squealed.

"No," Charlie said. "S'a nine. That means an extra card."

"Three means a extra card," I said.

"No, three is wild. Four matches the pot."

"Where's the vodka?"

"So, match the pot."

"This's a nine, not a three."

"Then make it wild. Do something."

"Where's the vodka?"

"I'll take an extra card."

"Okay, take two."

"No, one's enough."

"Go ahead, take two. What the hell. Go ahead."

"Okay, I'll take two. But I insis' you all take one, then. Go ahead. Here'sh…here's one for you, Ed, and you Blake…say, what'sh your name, Blake?"

"Blake."

"Oh, sure."

"I mean your firs' name."

"Oh. Joshua. Joshua."

"Josh-yuh fit the battle of Jericho," Ed said, and we all laughed. We kept on laughing while Charlie dealt Ed his next card, a jack.

"Jack. What's a jack do?"

"Nothin'."

"Has to do somethin'. Ma'shes the pot, I think."

"No, doubles the pot."

"Okay, put in a five, we'll call it square."

"Sure, but gimme an extra card."

"Okay."

"Here, have some vodka."

"Thanks."

"Shoot."

"A deuce. A deuce does somethin', I know. A deuce gets somethin', I think."

"A extra card."

"No. We each give Josh a nickel, that's it. Deuces get a nickel. Jesus, thi'sh a good game, huh?"

The deck ran out before we'd completed the fourth round. By this time, Ed had eleven extra cards, I had seven, and Charlie had thirteen. There was, according to our last count, thirty dollars and fourteen cents in the pot. We showed our hands.

Charlie had a royal flush and five aces.

I had six queens and a high straight.

Ed had nine queens and two pair, aces and jacks.

We couldn't decide who won, so we split the pot between us and started another round. We also killed the bottle of vodka, and when Ed discovered there wasn't another bottle in the cabinet, we opened a fifth of gin. We forgot the cards at about midnight and began singing all the old songs we knew, most of them dirty. Charlie was a fine baritone, and Ed had a nice tenor voice. We sang and we drank, and by one-thirty we were all on the floor, and none of us could lift the fifth of rye which we'd opened after the gin ran out.

By one-thirty-one, we were all unconscious.

I came to at three-fifteen.

I looked at the dial of my watch, and I rolled over, thinking there was still a lot of time before I had to be at the office. I rolled into something hard, and I reached under me for it and discovered it was an empty bottle.

I held the bottle up and tried to focus on it.

Bottle, bottle, now what the hell was a bottle doing in my bed? I got up and started to swing my legs over the side of the bed when I discovered there was no bed there at all. The walls were slanting peculiarly and somebody in the vicinity reeked like a distillery. I belched and realized I was the one who was doing the reeking, and that struck me funny, so I started to giggle. I got to my feet unsteadily and wobbled across the room.

Two guys were lying on the floor, and I figured, Man, this was one hell of a party, but it's time to go home.

I looked for my hat, decided finally that I hadn't come with one, and then went outside to the Buick.

Only the Buick wasn't there, so I figured some dumb bastard had taken the car by mistake and left me his Olds. Same company, I thought. General Motors, so here we go, General. I climbed in behind the wheel, thankful that the dumb bastard had left the keys in the ignition. Well, we'd straighten it all out in the morning. In the meantime, I was really…

Party.

Party!

I was sober in a tenth of a second.

I slapped the car into reverse and gunned it back against the house. Then I rammed it into drive, let the hydramatic take over, and raced for Cam Stewart's house.

10.

Gunsmoke Acres, the big white pillars said. Gunsmoke Acres, and I turned the nose of that Olds into the gravel driveway, rammed the accelerator down into Whirlaway, shooting around the curves, watching the greys and blacks and whites speed by in the darkness.

I pulled up outside the garage, and jammed on the brakes.

The house was dark.

I climbed out of the car and figured the party was now in its nude-in-the-swimming-pool stage, so I headed straight for the back of the house. There was still no light and no noise, and no nothing to give indication of a party. I began cursing myself for having missed the boat. I glanced at the luminous dial of my watch and saw that it was three-forty-eight. Hell, everybody was probably home in bed.

I walked around back and the place was deserted. The swimming pool glistened like black oil in the darkness. I stood at its edge and looked over the empty beach chairs, the empty patio, the empty everything.

"You planning on a swim, Josh?" the voice said.

I whirled abruptly.

She was sitting in the shadow of the house, sitting far back in a deep beach chair. Most of her was in darkness, with the moonlight gleaming on her long legs and leaving the rest of her in shadows, snug in the pocket of the chair.

"Cam?" I asked.

"The water's cold," she said. "I should know."

"You been in?"

"Couldn't think of a quicker way to sober up. Where were you, Josh? I missed you."

I walked over to where she was sitting, watching the moonlight play on her long legs, wishing it would splash onto the rest of her. Cam Stewart in a bathing suit was something to see. I envied the warm pocket of the chair.

"How was the party?" I asked.

"Nice. Very nice. Everybody got drunk, and there was nary a rape."

"Did you sign?" I asked anxiously.

"I signed."

"That's too bad."

"Why?"

"I'll have to sue. You, and Becker, and maybe even Rutherford, for handling the deal. You're infringing."

"Oh, infringement, nuts. That's what your partner said, too."

"When was this?"

"When he was up here. Before he got shot. I told him I didn't even remember signing any damned agreement, and he told me I'd better remember fast because infringement, infringement, infringement."

"He was right."

"He was right." Cam shrugged, or at least the movement in the darkness of the chair must have been a shrug. "Where were you, Josh? I thought you'd be here."

"You don't know, huh?"

"Why, no."

"Well, someone sure as hell knows. If it's not you, it's Becker or Rutherford. I was kidnaped."

"Oh, not really." She began chuckling, and then she uncrossed her legs and pulled them close to her chest, leaving only her ankles and toes in the moonlight, the rest of her still cloaked in the deep blackness of the shadows and the chair.

"Yes, really."

"Were you injured?"

"No. My abductors turned out to be two very nice guys who apparently had orders not to harm me. Their job was to keep me away from this party. They succeeded very well."

"How?"

"We all got roaring drunk."

"Well, good," Cam said. She laughed again, stretching her legs into the moonlight. She sank further into the chair, and more of her legs showed, and I wondered just how brief that bathing suit was. "We got roaring drunk, too."

"Sure, but you sobered up in the pool. I sobered by remembering your party. There's a difference."

"Go ahead," she said. "Use the pool. No one in it now."

"I haven't a suit."

"You don't need one," she said. And then, so softly that I almost didn't hear it, "I seldom use one."

I had risen and was heading for the pool when it registered. I wasn't going to go swimming, of course. I just wanted another look at it. What she said stopped me short, and I turned to face her. She was sitting in the deep pocket of the chair, but she was leaning forward now, and her upper half was in the moonlight, too.

The moonlight slanted down and kissed her naked breasts, bathing the full curves of her body in molten silver. She was cleanly built, with full, flowing curves, strong and young. She tilted her head now, and the moonlight touched her face and her mouth and her throat.

"I was waiting for you, Josh," she said. "I've been waiting all night."

I stood on the edge of the pool for a moment, and then I walked to her slowly, and she came up out of the chair to meet me.

I took her hands, and we stood like that for a moment, just our hands locked. And then she lifted her face again, standing on tiptoe, and I took her into my arms.

Her flesh was still cold from the water, but her lips were warm and moist, and she moved closer to me, and her arms tightened around my neck. She moved her mouth gently, but there was an insistent pressure in her lips, and in the slim, cool length of her body pressed against mine.

I tangled my hand in her hair and I pulled her face back and kissed the dark hollow of her throat, her shoulders…

I lifted her, then, and carried her to the long chaise longue near the pool's edge. I put her down on the soft cushions, and her body was a dull ivory against the deep blue of the fabric.

"I'm sorry about the agreement, Josh," she said softly. "I'm sorry you lost out."

"That's all right," I said.

"I'm truly sorry. Truly." She paused, and then pulled me to her breast, holding me tightly, almost fiercely.

"I'll make it up to you, Josh. I'll make it up to you."

11.

I left Gunsmoke Acres at noon the next day. I left Cam in her large bed, with satin sheets pulled to her throat, with the young firm lines of her body sculpting the sheets. She smiled up at me lazily, and then lifted one arm to wave, and the sheet fell free of one breast, and I sure as hell did not want to leave.

I tried to kiss her hastily, aiming for her cheek, but she pulled my face down to hers, and when she kissed me, it curled my toes, I left, though. I left because I still wanted to pull this deal out of the fire, and I wasn't going to do that by dallying with Cam Stewart.

I thought of the deal all the way back to the city. The rain had cooled things considerably, and there was a briskness in the air that was reminiscent of autumn. Perversely, I wished for the heat again. And I thought. I'd have to call Mike, of course. Still, I hated to drag this damned thing into the courts. Once that happened, there'd be calendar delays and haggling and waiting and I'd be sixty-five before a commission rolled into the agency.

I had a hunch they'd try to settle out of court if I could produce the agreement. They'd be crazy not to. But I didn't have the agreement, and no amount of wishing would bring it back. Well, maybe Mike could figure something. He was on a retainer, and that's what he got paid for. I'd have felt a lot better if Cam Stewart weren't involved in the deal.

It's one thing to take a perfect stranger to court, but it's another to sue someone you know, and I knew Cam well, very well. She had been something to remember, all right. Something you lock away and pull out on rainy days. Something to mull over in the quiet of a room at dusk, when the shadows begin to lengthen and the city night noises begin outside your window. Yesterday's gardenia, you know. That sort of thing. A perfect memory that you want to keep.

You wonder about things like that. A casual piece is a casual piece, and I've never been one to make it more than that. Christ only knew how many times Cam Stewart had rolled in the hay, and with how many men. Those scenes in her books weren't all imagination, I decided.

But there'd been something else there, too, something more than a wham-bam-thank-you-ma'am. Maybe you'd call it love. That something where eyes speak, or the pressure of a hand. Where every motion sort of fits, like the intricate parts of a ballet. It happens sometimes, and it can happen with a slut in Panama, or with your wife, or with a casual pick-up in a Broadway bar. It can happen, and there's honest love while it's happening. Not just the physical drive, and not just the enjoyment, the animal enjoyment of body with body. Something more than that. Something that somehow separates two people from every other person in the world, for just a little while. It happens, and the two people are very rarely consciously aware of it, or grateful for it. They simply know within themselves that it's happened, and they hold the memory gently, like a quietly shimmering ball of crystal.

Sometimes you can't go back. Not with the memory fresh on your mind and body. The memory is so keen, so poignant, that everything following it is dull and commonplace in comparison. It might be that way with Cam, and I hoped it wouldn't.

I hoped it wouldn't because I'd liked her, and I'd loved her there a while back; I'd loved her very much.

And you don't sue people you love, I thought. Unless a hell of a lot of money is riding on it. There was a hell of a lot of money riding on this.

I'd sure sue if I had to. I'd sue, and if the memory would be all I got out of it, that would be enough. I'd hold the memory, taking it out and cherishing it occasionally, remembering what could have been—or maybe what could never have been.

The things that never can be are sometimes more exquisite than those that can, and are, and always will be.

I drove slowly, with a great peace inside me, I smelled the clean air, and I felt the breeze on my face, and I was sorry when the drive was over and I came into the city. I left the car in a garage and walked to the office, trying to bring my mind back to what had to be done now. There was a lot that had to be done now, and I wanted Mike's advice before I went ahead.

My first impulse was to call the papers, of course, and get them to splash the story all over their pages in heavy black print. Following Becker's announcement, that would really come as a jolt. I'd have to ask Mike.

I walked into the reception room and straight over to where Jeanette sat behind her switchboard.

"Honey," I said, "get Mike Solowitz for me, will you?"

"Yes, Mr. Blake." She looked up, wide-eyed. "Oh, good morning, Mr. Blake."

"Good morning, Jeanette. It's afternoon, though, honey."

She smiled prettily. "I'll get Mr. Solowitz for you, sir."

I went into my office and waited for Jeanette to buzz me with the call. I lighted a cigarette, made myself comfortable, and then lifted the receiver.

"Hello, Mike. This is Josh."

"Afternoon, Josh. What can I do for you?" Mike Solowitz was a dyspeptic kind of guy whom I'd never seen smile. He had a long face and a carefully trimmed mustache. His eyes were shrewdly intelligent, and there was a bullying look about his mouth that scared juries into casting their votes his way.

"The Cam Stewart mess again," I said.

"I saw the papers, Josh."

"Well, what now?"

"That's a good question. Why didn't you show them the agreement?"

"It's gone, Mike. Both copies. That's why."

"Mmm."

"So?"

"So you're up the creek without a paddle." I could picture Mike grimacing on the other end of the line. "If you want me to start suit, I will. Maybe the agreements will turn up before the thing gets to court. You can't hope for any kind of quick settlement without them, though."

"I was thinking of scaring them into settlement, Mike."

"How?"

"Release the story to the press."

"What good will that do?"

"Well, they'll realize we're not playing games. They'll…"

"Josh, if the thing has gone this far, they're not playing games either. They obviously think you haven't got any agreement. Or else they don't give a damn. This can be honesty on their part, or it can be a squeeze play designed to force you out of the picture. Either way, I'm sure they're not playing games either, Josh."

"You'd advise against giving the newspapers the story, Mike?"

"Yes."

"Why?"

"It won't help your case any. The only thing it'll do is give them extra publicity. You should see the spread they got this morning. That first movie is getting more publicity than Pearl

Harbor did. If you want to help their cause along, go ahead."

"You're forgetting, Mike."

"What?"

"That I get twenty-five percent of the movie proceeds if we can salvage this one."

"If. If we lose, you're left with a dirty stick, and they still get the free publicity."

"That's a calculated risk, isn't it?"

"It's a risk, but I don't know how calculated it is. Look, Josh, face the situation. As long as you can't get your hands on that agreement, you haven't a leg to stand on. All we can do is stall around until the agreement shows up. Damn it, you should have taken better care of it."

"Christ, we had a stat made!"

"You should have had *ten* made! On something like this, you don't take foolish chances."

"All right, I've learned my lesson."

"Good."

"But I think even ten stats wouldn't have made any difference. I think Del was killed for the original of that agreement, Mike."

"Oh, horse manure."

"That's what I think."

"Maybe you're right. I've prosecuted murder cases in my day, though, and it all sounds too complicated. Most murders aren't so scientifically motivated, Josh. Simple motives, usually."

"You sound like someone I know."

"He must be a very smart man," Mike said drily.

"So what do we do?"

"I'll start suit. Then we pray that the agreement turns up. If it doesn't, you'll have to sell a million pulp stories to make up the lost commission on this one."

"Don't I know it."

"Yeah. Okay, Josh, anything else?"

"Nothing I can think of."

"Send one of your kids over with all the information I'll need. Names, dates, all that. I'll contact their lawyers and maybe we can work something out, I doubt it, though. I'll probably have to sue."

"I'll leave it to you, Mike."

"Fine. So long Josh, I'm piled up."

"Right. So long, Mike."

I hung up, and then I stubbed out my cigarette and leaned back in the chair. Mike was right, of course. We should have had ten stats made of the agreement. Hell, we should have had ten dozen made. We should have thought of it. Del or I, or both of us. We hadn't, and that was tough, but the agreement was gone, and I could whistle now.

The buzzer on my desk sounded, and I clicked the toggle.

"Yes."

"Are you taking calls, Mr. Blake?" Jeanette asked.

"Who is it, Jeanette?"

"Mr. Phelps at Tarrance."

"Who?"

"Mr. Phelps."

"Okay, I'll take it. What's he on?"

"Eight, sir."

"Thank you."

I pressed the extension button, lifted the receiver, and said, "Hello?"

"Mr. Blake?"

"Yes."

"This is Jim Phelps at Tarrance. I don't believe we've ever talked to each other, Mr. Blake."

"No," I said.

"I've just been taken on, and I'll be doing a lot of the preliminary science-fiction reading, I thought we might get better acquainted."

"That's a good idea," I said. I was instantly on guard. I sure as hell did not want to have lunch with a snot-nose straight out of Harvard.

"How about lunch some time next week?"

"Well, just a moment, let me check my calendar." I covered the mouthpiece with one hand and then leaned back in my chair while I went through an imaginary calendar. After a few minutes, I uncovered the mouthpiece and said, "Nope, I'm afraid next week is out. Just a moment." I paused while I leafed through some more imaginary pages. "Gosh, I seem to be tied up for the next three weeks. We're in the middle of a rather big movie deal, you see."

"I see," Phelps said.

"I would like to get together, though. Very much," I lied. "Suppose I give you a call as soon as this deal is concluded, and we can make an appointment then?"

Phelps brightened. "That sounds fine."

"Good. Let me just make a note of that." I pretended to pick up a non-existent pencil. "Call Mr. Phelps," I said very slowly, as if I were pacing the words to match the imaginary writing I was doing on a figmental scrap of paper. "At Tarrance. There."

"Fine, fine. And in the meantime…"

"We'll keep the stuff coming, of course."

"On this one yarn we have here—*Big Boys.*"

"Oh, yes. A fine story."

"Yes, it certainly has a lot to recommend it."

I waited.

"However…"

I waited.

"...the author has no real conception of Englishmen. I mean, I spent a good deal of time in England; got my Bachelor's at Oxford, in fact."

"Oh really?"

"Yes. And his conception of Englishmen is all off. His Englishmen are fully as bad as any British novelist's Americans."

"Perhaps he meant them to be bad," I said. "I think he was trying to satirize them. Give the American reader the stereotype of the Englishman. I don't think he was trying..."

"Yes, but his conception is all wrong."

I shrugged wearily. "I'll have the yarn picked up," I said.

"Would you? And please keep them coming. We're always in the market for science-fiction humor."

"If grimly," I said.

"I beg your pardon?"

"I was just making a note to have the yarn picked up."

"Oh, fine. Nice talking to you, Mr. Blake."

"The same here, Mr. Phelps. I'll be calling you soon."

"Fine, fine. Well, goodbye."

"Goodbye, Mr. Phelps."

I hung up and stared at the phone and wondered what the publishing business was coming to. I shook my head. A nice kid, Phelps, undoubtedly. Fresh out of college and so impressed with his first editorial job. The author of that yarn had written and sold some four hundred short stories and three novels. Phelps had written several term papers, and maybe a few one-act plays in a half-ass college course. The only thing he'd ever sold was probably a spot on the gym floor to an incoming freshman. But he was now an editor. He now had the right to say aye or nay to stories that came in. It would never cease to amaze me.

Reading enjoyment, no matter how you sliced it, was a purely personal thing. One editor's meat was another's poison. I'd seen assigned stories fail at low-pay, slow-pay markets, only to sell higher up the line for ten times what we would have gotten. It all depended on how Harry or Jake or Sam or Fred or Pete or Barnaby felt when he read the yarn. If his wife had served him cold eggs for breakfast, too bad about the story, even if it went on to win a Pulitzer Prize later. But if Fred had won ten dollars as door prize in his annual community get-together, by God, everything looked good. That was the time to unload all the crap.

Still, it seemed unfair. There should be a course for prospective editors—a yardstick. Something an author could go by, besides his own judgment—which was often wrong. I've seen writers turn out practically a carbon copy of a yarn that sold two months ago. We'd send the yarn to the very same market, and they'd send back a note, or make a call, saying it was not their type of stuff.

Did that mean the yarn was bad? Hell, no.

Did that mean the author was slipping? Christ, no.

Did that mean the publishing business was being revolutionized overnight? Perish the thought.

It simply meant the eggs had been cold that morning.

Which reminded me.

I buzzed Jeanette, and when she came on, I said, "Honey, order me some breakfast, will you?"

"Yes, sir. What would you like, Mr. Blake?"

"Orange juice, coffee, toast, a soft-boiled egg, and a jelly doughnut. Fast, please. I'm very hungry."

"Yes, sir."

I glanced at the mail on my desk and then rummaged through the neatly stacked, opened letters. I pulled a sheet from the pile at random.

It was from Stagg Bellew, the tough-guy writer with the Pekinese look.

Dear Josh;

You'll find herewith (unless that thieving bastard of a postmaster is slitting my envelopes again) a gem titled Call Me, Adam. *It features that dauntless private dick, Adam Addams, take him or leave him. It runs to 20,000 words, which is too long for most markets and too short for the majority, Which means it can be used to stuff the soles of your shoes. Please get three million pesos for it.*

I smiled and went on to the next paragraph.

In your letter of the 9th, you asked whether it was all right for Crest to change the title of my last novel. You also mention, and somewhat casually, you bastard, that they are buying the book and paying a $2,000 advance.

Now, this is the way I feel, Josh.

I like the title Sweet Violence. *To me, it is the sweetest little title in all this sweet wide world, bar none. The fact that they wish to change it to* My Flesh Is Warm *disturbs me no end. I would rather relinquish my life than my original title.*

But between us, Josh, grab that goddamned 2,000 bucks and grab it fast, and tell them they can change the goddamned title to My Vagina Is Magenta, *if they want to.*

Trusting you are the same,
Stagg

I put the letter down, sighed, thought *Writers,* and then wondered if I'd ever met one who was sane. My breakfast arrived at just about that time, so I didn't have to pursue the subject further. I paid and tipped the boy, and then started on my orange juice. It was good and cold, and I enjoyed it. The coffee was hot, and the toast and egg were both warm, and I ate with relish and was beginning to feel a little like myself. I polished off the main course and was starting on the jelly doughnut when the door flew open.

A jelly doughnut is a sloppy thing. This jelly doughnut was as sloppy as most, and it also had a liberal sprinkling of powdered sugar on it. I was holding it deftly, with my hands full of sugar, and the jelly about to drip into a large blob on my desk, and one bite of the doughnut in my mouth. That was precisely when the door opened.

The character standing in the doorway was David Gunnison. My first reaction was to throw the doughnut at his face and watch the jelly fly. I tried to say something, but the piece of dough in my mouth prevented any outburst. I thought about all the Davids I was having trouble with. The David Gunnisons, would-be writers, and the David Beckers, would-be producers. I began to feel a little like Goliath, so I swallowed the lump of dough quickly and shouted, "What the holy hell…"

"Steady," Gunnison said.

"Where's Jeanette? How'd you get through that reception room without being…"

"She went to the can. I waited for her to leave and then walked right in."

"You're a persistent bastard, aren't you, Gunnison?"

"Very."

There was still that crafty look in his farmer eyes, and I couldn't shake the idea that he had something important on his mind. Maybe Stagg's letter had put me in a good mood, or maybe I just wanted to finish my coffee and doughnut without being interrupted by a lot of fisticuffs. Or maybe it was that something-important look in his eyes. Whatever it was, I didn't run around the desk and throw him out the window.

"Your book again?" I asked.

"Yes."

"Gunnison, why don't you go directly to the publishers? There must be about eight million of them in New York alone. And then there's Chicago and Indiana and…"

"You don't stand a chance without an agent."

"Gunnison, your book won't stand a chance with or without an agent. I'm leveling with you; I'm being an honest guy. Take it and burn it. Hide it. Go away with it. Just leave me alone."

"No."

I sighed. "All right, no. Don't leave me alone. Sit down and pretend you're part of the furniture. Keep quiet and don't bother me and…"

"I've got something you want, Blake."

"Sure. So has every writer in the world."

"No. Just me. I think you'll be very interested in what I have."

"You've got a great talent, admittedly. For annoying people. Look, Gunnison, I'm being a nice guy. Up to now, we've wrestled every time we've met. This time, we're talking."

"That's right."

"Fine. That's the sensible way to do it. So, let me ask you once more to go, far away, far, far away where the swallows bide. Go, Gunnison. *Adios.* Goodbye. So long."

Gunnison reached into his jacket pocket and took out a neatly folded piece of paper. "I copied this one," he said. "I've got the original, though."

"Plagiarism…"

"Read it," he said, thrusting it across the desk.

I reached for the single sheet of paper, expecting a poem he'd lifted from the *Saturday Evening Post,* something inspirational perhaps, or something witty. Something more to bother me with. I unfolded it once, and then I unfolded it again, and then my eyes almost popped out of my head when I started reading the pica type.

Gentlemen:

Thank you for your recent letter. This will grant you permission to handle exclusively the radio and television rights to all the published novels bearing my byline, provided a $500 option is paid within the next week. It is understood that you are the only agency acting in this capacity. Good luck.

Sincerely,

Between the *Sincerely* and the signature, Gunnison had typed in the parenthesized: *(signed)*.

And under that: *CAM STEWART.*

It was the goods, all right. It was the agreement word for word, and I stared at it, and managed to stammer, "Where… where…where…"

"I've got the original," Gunnison said. "That is, I've got a photostat of the original."

"But, where? How…"

"You'll be angry."

"No, just tell me…" And then I realized, and I did begin to get angry, but I held the anger in check. This was only a copy, and it wasn't signed. If Gunnison had the signed stat, I wanted it, and getting angry wouldn't help me any.

"You were the guy who slugged me," I said. "Outside Lydia Rafney's place."

"Yes," Gunnison said softly.

"Why? Why the hell…"

"I was sore. I didn't like the way you threw me out of here. I waited downstairs, followed you, and then got a cab and found out where you lived."

"So you were the guy in the cab?"

"Yes."

"Go on."

"I kept an eye on you, then. I was really sore. I wanted to beat the hell out of you. When you went to that swank apartment, I followed you there, and I waited outside in the hall. I was getting sorer every minute."

So was I but I didn't show it.

"Go on," I said.

"When you came out, you were putting something into your wallet. I hit you and then I made sure you were out."

"By kicking me."

"Well, I guess I did kick you," Gunnison said sheepishly. "I was sore."

"Go on."

"I saw this paper that fell out of your hands, and I picked it up out of curiosity. After I read it, I knew it was something big, something I could bargain with. Hell, everybody knows Cam Stewart."

"So you figured a little blackmail…"

"Just a fair trade," Gunnison corrected quickly. "I've still got the stat. If it's important to you, you can have it back. Provided…"

"Provided what?"

"Provided you take my book on for marketing."

"Where's your book?"

"Outside. You'll take it on?"

"Damn right I will. Where's the stat?"

"I've got it right here. In my wallet."

"Let me see it."

Gunnison shook his head. "Uh-uh. I want a contract first. A signed piece of paper saying you'll do your best to sell my book, expend every effort. You know."

"All right, fine. Fine."

"I'll go get the book."

He went out of the office, and I swung my portable up from

under the desk and typed out some nonsense about expending
my best efforts to sell his goddamned novel. I was excited, really
excited. This would sew up the deal. I typed fast, and by the time
I was through, Gunnison was back with the novel. He plunked
it down on my desk.

"There," he said.

"Fine. Here's your contract."

Gunnison picked up the rubbish I'd typed and read it carefully, nodding all the way. "Uh…" he said.

"Yes."

"Just to make sure. I mean, just to be certain you go all out for
the book."

"Yeah?"

"I'd like an advance against its future sale."

"What?"

Gunnison nodded solemnly.

"How much?" I asked.

"Three hundred. That's the usual advance, isn't it?"

I didn't answer.

"You can deduct your ten percent," Gunnison said generously.
"Make it for two-seventy. This is just to make you try harder, you
understand."

"Sure, I understand." I fished my personal checkbook out of
my inside jacket pocket, and wrote out the check. "Here."

Gunnison waved the check in the air to dry the ink. "Thanks."

"The photostat, please."

"Oh, yes."

He took out his wallet and handed me the folded stat. I unfolded it hastily. It was the stat, all right—beautiful, with Cam
Stewart's signature on it as plain as day.

"Okay, Gunnison," I said. "Scram."

"We're author and agent now," he said.

"Right. I'll call you if there's any good news."

I ran to the intercom and buzzed Jeanette. She came on, and I said, "Get me Mike Solowitz, baby."

"Yes, sir."

"Is he an editor?" Gunnison asked.

"No, he's a lawyer. Goodbye, Gunnison. I'll contact you."

He stood in the doorway, undecided for a moment, and wondering perhaps if I wasn't calling a lawyer because of the nifty blackmail he'd just pulled.

"Well, all right," he said at last, and then he left, closing the door behind him.

You sonovabitch, I thought after him.

The buzzer sounded.

"Yes?"

"Mr. Solowitz on seven."

"Thank you." I lifted the phone. "Hello, Mike."

"What now, Josh?"

"I've got the agreement."

"What? Who…"

"The bastard who stole it returned it. It's a stat, but clear as mud."

"Good. Send it over."

"Uh-uh, baby. This isn't leaving my hands again. I'll bring it over. But first, I have a visit to make."

"Who?"

"Cam Stewart."

"Why?"

"She's sensible. Once I show her the agreement, she'll realize she's pulled a boner. She'll call off the hounds. We're in, Mike."

"It looks that way."

"It sure as hell does."

"Okay, good luck. Let me know what happens."

"I will. So long."

I hung up and pulled on a jacket, making sure that the stat

was in my wallet and buttoned in my pocket. I walked over to Jeanette and said, "If anyone calls, I'm out to see Cam Stewart, honey."

"All right."

One of the switchboard lights went on at that moment, and I waited to see if the call was an important one. Jeanette plugged in and said, "Gilbert and Blake, good afternoon."

She listened, and I waited, and then she said, "Mr. Donato, sir."

"Who?"

"Mr. Donato. He's been calling every half hour, practically. He says those…"

"Tell him to call back, honey. This is important."

I walked out of the office, took the elevator down, and then got the Oldsmobile from the garage I'd left it in. I'd put in a call from Cam's place on the Buick, and the highway police had promised to deliver it there as soon as they located it. It gave me an excuse to visit her again, if I'd needed one. In the meantime, I was using the car belonging to Charlie and Ed, or whoever had hired them. It was a nice car, the Olds, and I almost regretted having to return it eventually.

I drove fast this time. The roads weren't wet or slippery, and it was a little too early for the suburban going-home traffic. I drove with the stat in my pocket and a big smile on my face, I was ready to set this deal on its feet, and I was also going to see Cam again, and that made me feel better than anything else. She was a remarkable woman—the kind you run across maybe five times in a lifetime, if you're lucky. I drove, and anticipation rose within me, and I almost didn't think of the stat until I was very close to Gunsmoke Acres.

Something of its significance penetrated, then.

I hadn't been slugged for the stat.

I'd been slugged because one of the crazier writers, David Gunnison by name, had a grudge. He'd taken it out on me, unfortunately recognizing the importance of the stat at the same time.

An accident, pure and simple. David Gunnison was simply a red herring, the reddest herring I'd ever encountered.

I began to realize how tough Di Luca's job really was. How do you pick a murderer? How do you distinguish the significant things from those that are unimportant, especially when the unimportant ones look significant? Life has no rules. Neither does murder. Gunnison didn't even know my partner had been killed. He had his own personal motivation, and he followed it. He wanted to beat up a guy who'd made him sore. So he followed the guy in a cab, and then kept a close surveillance on him, and when the time was ripe, *bop!* Unfortunately, I was the guy who'd been bopped. And, unfortunately, I'd been holding the stat in my hand when the roof fell in. Gunnison had picked up the stat, still oblivious of any murder, had recognized it as something that would help his particular cause, and had used it.

But I'd assumed I'd been slugged by someone interested in getting the stat. In fact, I'd assumed the murderer had slugged me.

I'd been wrong, and Gunnison could have been a red herring if you looked at it that way. But things aren't always as simple as Di Luca made them out to be. As long as there were people, there would be complications. There was no pattern, except in mystery novels.

Which meant that Del may *not* have been killed for the original of the agreement.

I wasn't buying that. I still felt that the two were tangled, and the fact that Gunnison hadn't been involved meant nothing. I couldn't see any other reason, nor could I see a reason for the holes in Lydia, and it was really a good thing I wasn't connected with the police department. That was Di Luca's headache, and he was welcome to it.

Me, I had a stat in my pocket, and a deal in that same pocket, and a girl waiting for me at the other end of the line. And what a girl!

I pulled in between the twin white pillars, and sped up the gravel driveway. The place was very quiet, with only the sounds of the insects humming on the air.

I drove to the garage and saw my Buick parked there. I stepped out of the Olds, checked my own car for damage, satisfied when the broken window and wet upholstery seemed to be the only casualties.

I was wasting time.

Cam was inside.

I was sure as hell wasting time.

I went to the front door and lifted the monogrammed knocker. I waited for a few moments, and then the door opened wide, and the undertaker stood there, only he wasn't grinning this time. He looked very sad, which is befitting an undertaker, even when he's really a butler.

"Hi, kid," I said. "Miss Stewart home?"

He blinked at me, and his eyes were cavernous and sad, and I felt so damned happy that his sadness looked ten times as sad.

"Hey," I said, "snap out of it. Is Miss Stewart home?"

He blinked once more, and then his voice came, deep and lonely, like the voice of a ghost in a vacuum.

"Miss Stewart is dead, sir," he said.

12.

I stood there with the insect sounds humming around me, and I looked at the sad-eyed, sad-faced butler, and somehow my undertaker metaphor wasn't funny anymore.

He'd made it come true, and I just stood there and looked at him with my mouth open and my eyes blinking. He nodded solemnly, still experiencing his own shock, and able to understand a little of mine.

"I've called the police, sir," he said. "They should be here soon."

I followed him into the house, and then into the long living room that ran across the rear wall. The drapes were drawn back, and I could see the swimming pool and the patio through the floor-to-ceiling windows of the room.

Cam lay in front of one window. She wore a playsuit that was a sort of rompers affair—a high dog-collar neck, and bunched bloomers that hugged her tanned thighs. The front of the suit was a soggy mass of blood. It clung limply to her breast, and the blood ran onto the floor beneath her. A broken glass was on the floor, its amber liquid uniting with the blood, forming a muddy pool.

The window behind her was a crooked mass of broken shards.

"When…when did this happen?" I asked. I turned away from her because I couldn't look anymore. Death had really hit hard this time; very hard. This time it was a personal loss, and I felt drained, empty.

"I'd gone to the village, sir," the butler told me. "Just to pick up a few things. When I returned…" He didn't finish. He just shook his head, and I unconsciously shook mine with him. It was very quiet in the room.

"Was anyone with her when you left?"

"Yes, sir."

"Who?"

"Mr. Becker, sir."

"He was here? With Cam?"

"Yes, sir."

David Becker. The little moon-faced producer, Could a little man like him do a big thing like this? I wondered, and I looked at Cam's lifeless body again.

"What time did he get here?" I asked.

"Shortly after you left this morning, sir. At about twelve-thirty, I would say."

"And he stayed all afternoon?"

"Yes, sir. They were discussing the details of the motion picture, I believe."

"Did they argue, or anything?"

"No, sir."

A little of the shock was wearing off, and it was being replaced by a gnawing wonder. Why Cam? I mean, if the movie deal was all-important, why kill the author? If Del was killed to get the original agreement, and if Lydia was killed for Christ only knew what reason, where did Cam fit into the murder scheme? Was it that she was no longer necessary, now that the contracts had been inked? Would the publicity on her murder help the picture?

Or had she changed her mind? Had she told Becker she suddenly remembered the agreement, and wanted me in on the deal? Was that it?

I was confused. I was honestly baffled, and I wished Di Luca were there because I needed someone with a cold mind and a deadpan face.

"Which police did you call?" I asked.

"The local police, sir."

"Mind if I use the phone?"

"Not at all, sir."

I called Di Luca, and he took the news very calmly. He told me it was out of his jurisdiction, but since it tied in with the earlier deaths—or *possibly* tied in with them—he'd be right over. He asked me to wait, and I thanked him and then hung up.

When I heard a car outside, I thought it was the Connecticut police. I went outside in time to see a taxi stop in front of the house. The side door opened and Carlyle Rutherford got out, paying the driver, and then waving an arm at me.

I waved back and watched him walk up to the house.

"Hello, Blake," he said.

"Rutherford," I acknowledged.

He grinned broadly, and then looked over to the garage, where I'd parked the Olds behind my Buick.

"I see you returned my car," he said.

"Your…" I stopped short and then said, "So it was your party last night."

Rutherford's grin widened. "One smart-angle boy against another, Blake. The boys tell me you had quite a time."

"Quite a time."

An anxious look crossed his rugged features. "They didn't harm you, did they?"

"No, they were very genial."

"You're not sore, are you?"

"It was pretty dirty, Rutherford."

"No dirtier than a lot I've seen. You'd have done the same, Blake."

"Maybe. I doubt it."

"You'd have done the same," he said firmly.

"Maybe we're just not in the same league, Rutherford. Maybe

you're carrying this fraternity-of-smart-angle-boys idea too far."

Rutherford shrugged. "I had to keep you away from the party."

"It doesn't matter anymore, Rutherford. I've got the agreement, and you can see it any time you want to."

Rutherford's mouth fell open, and he let his big hands drop to his sides. I guess he really believed that no agreement had existed, because the shock on his face was plainly evident. I still hadn't told him Cam was dead. If he knew, he was going to have a hell of a time looking surprised. And if he didn't know, I wanted to see his reaction. In my own mind, I'd discounted him as the murderer the moment I'd learned the Olds was his. It's a little hard for a man to move around freely when he hasn't got a car. The fact that he'd arrived just now in a cab seemed to indicate he didn't own a second car. Still, I wanted to see his face when he learned Cam was dead.

"You've got it, huh?"

"Yes."

"May I see it?"

"Sure." I fished out the agreement, unfolded it, and held it where he could read it plainly. I did not let it out of my hands.

Rutherford read it slowly and carefully, then shook his head sadly. "Mmm," he said. Then: "That settles that, I guess."

"Except for a few details."

"Like what?"

"Come on inside, Rutherford."

Rutherford shrugged. He was too good a businessman to let a little setback knock him for a loop. "Where's Cam?" he asked, looking over his shoulder.

"Inside," I said. "Come on."

He followed me in, and I led him to the living room. He was still peering over his shoulder, looking for Cam, believing—or trying to give the impression he believed—she was outside.

She was not outside. She was still sprawled before the broken window, and Rutherford had not seen her. He gave one last look through the open door, and then, turning his head, said, at the same time, "Well, where is she?"

"Right there," I said.

He turned his head sharply, and then he saw her.

He was either a very good actor, or he was honestly surprised. I watched his face, and it was not a pleasant thing to see. He looked at the body, and somehow it didn't register. He kept turning his head, and then snapped it back in a double-take that would have been comical were it not for the expression accompanying it.

His crooked eyebrows shot up onto his forehead, and his thin lips popped open. His eyes were suddenly stabbed with pain, and then his face creased into a thousand anguished wrinkles, and he did a curious thing for a man as big as he was. He brought his heavy hands up close to his chest. The fingers interlocked, and he wrung them like an old woman watching a funeral procession. He kept wringing his hands, and he still hadn't said a word, and then the tears sprang into his eyes—real tears that clouded the brown and then spilled over onto his cheeks.

He walked to her slowly, and he stood looking down at her, still not saying a word, still wringing his big hands. When he turned to me, he was still crying soundlessly. He dropped his hands, and said softly, "That was dirty, Blake. That was dirtier than I've ever been."

I thought he was referring to the death, at first, and then I realized he meant the way I'd broken the news to him. Maybe it had been dirty, but I was in a dirty mood, and murder is as dirty as you can get.

"The police are on their way," I said.

"Who did it?"

"You tell me, Rutherford."

"You don't think…Jesus Christ, you surely don't think…"

"I don't know what to think."

He was suddenly angry. He clenched those big hands, and his lips formed a tight line across his face. "If I find the sonovabitch…"

"We may not have far to look," I said. "Becker was here a little while ago."

"Becker? He wouldn't…you're crazy if you think he would…" He seemed unable to say the word, and finally it came out. "…kill Cam. He…"

We heard the siren outside then, and we both shut up and went to greet the Connecticut police.

They asked a lot of questions, more questions than a man should be forced to answer in a lifetime. They were very thorough. They went through the place with a fine comb, taking pictures, lifting prints, marking the floor. And always the questions.

I was glad when Di Luca finally showed up. He had a short talk with the local detective, explaining his connection with the case. They seemed to get along well, and I watched silently, with all the confusion of activity around me.

Di Luca got his own men to work, and I admired the way they unobtrusively geared in with the work the Connecticut men were doing. Di Luca hovered over them for a while, making sure his orders were carried out, and then he walked over to where I was standing. There was no antagonism in his voice or his face now. He just looked very tired.

"Another one, Blake," he said.

I nodded.

"You knew her, huh?"

"I knew her."

"A damn shame. A very pretty girl."

"Yes."

"Looks like a .45, from what I could tell."

I nodded.

"We'll know for sure later. Snap out of it, Blake," he said suddenly.

"I'm sorry. I…"

"Sure, I know. It's not nice, no matter how you slice it. It's worse when it's someone you know and like."

"Yes."

"You still think that agreement is causing all these deaths, Blake?"

"I don't know."

"It's not, believe me."

"How do you know?"

"The pattern. It comes absurd after a while. It doesn't hang together. If the movie deal were the motivating factor, the killer wouldn't murder this way."

"I have one copy of the agreement now," I said dully. "The one that was stolen from me."

"Oh? Who stole it?"

"Gunnison. The writer…"

"Yeah. You should have told me this sooner, Blake."

"I only got the photostat just before I came up here."

"Is that why you came? To show the agreement to Miss Stewart?"

"Yes."

"What about the original?"

"It's still missing."

"I gave a lot of thought to your theory, you know. Before I threw it out of the window. It made some sense. A big deal was pending, and one of the leading parties to the deal is killed.

And an agreement is missing from the safe. That makes sense. Not too much sense, but sense enough to consider. And then Lydia Rafney was killed, and I revised my thinking and dropped that agreement angle completely."

"Is that why you booked me?"

"Yes. Yes, I began thinking along other lines. I figured maybe you were hot for Rafney, killed your partner because he was getting all the potatoes, and then killed her because she wouldn't come across even after he was dead."

"Simple motives."

"Sure."

"Why'd you let me go?"

"Hell, you heard the autopsy report. You couldn't have killed her. Speculation is one thing, Blake. Facts are another. The smart cop combines the two."

"And what about this?" I gestured toward Cam's shrouded body.

"This may make things a little clearer. It may tie in with another line of thought I had."

"What's that?"

"Del Gilbert was a big bastard, right?"

"I suppose."

"I checked around the field. I haven't been sitting on my dead duff. I found enough people who hated him to form a club. A big club. That made it harder, Blake. When there's so much hatred, there's motivation everywhere. But hatred alone isn't enough. Hatred can smolder and grow for a long time, but it will hardly ever force the average guy to kill, unless there's a sudden push. Say Gilbert had been screwing up one editor constantly, getting him in dutch with the publisher. All right, the editor hates him, hates him viciously, but not enough to break the highest law of Man. Then let's say Gilbert causes the guy to lose his job. There's the push that's needed. The editor is over the line now, and killing is a simple thing, motivated by an intense hatred."

"Del had a lot of guys fired," I said.

"I know, Blake. I checked on that, too. I discounted most of them as past the danger point. Once the spark comes, that's the time to kill. That's when any man can kill—any man. A butcher, or a baker, or a sexton. But the average man does not kill. He allows the spark to flash for a second, or an hour, or maybe a week. And then it burns itself out, dissipates itself. The time to kill is gone. He won't kill if he hasn't already."

"Then why all these murders? Assuming someone was pushed to the danger point by something that happened…why Lydia? And why Cam?"

"Lydia may have been a further reaction of the first death. At least, that's the way I figure it. The momentum of the first spark, if you will. Miss Stewart? It's hard to say, and it baffles me a little. Something else must have happened, something to rekindle that spark. You see, the sequence of murder is important, Blake. Once that spark is kindled, it must have direction. There must be a murder object. The object is not chosen at random. For example, if I'd been building up a hatred for you, when that hatred reached the danger point, I wouldn't go out and kill the neighborhood grocer. No, I'd kill you. First, anyway. So Del Gilbert was killed first."

"And then Lydia."

"Then Lydia. Maybe the hatred was not yet satisfied. Maybe the killer figured Gilbert wasn't enough. So Lydia was the next victim."

"That doesn't explain Cam."

"Maybe it does. That's the loophole in my reasoning, Blake. If I can figure why Miss Stewart was killed…" Di Luca shrugged.

"I'll find it. I'll find it, Blake. I don't think there'll be any more killing. I think the spark has gone out, and unless something happens to rekindle it, we're all right. By that time, I'll have my killer."

"Get him, Di Luca," I said.

"I've been trying to." He smiled thinly, and then said, "I think you'd better go home. Get a little rest. This is what I get paid for."

I thanked him and then started out. Rutherford was outside the house, sitting in the center of a ring of reporters. His grief seemed to have passed very rapidly. I walked back to where Rutherford held court. I broke through the ring of reporters and said, "I'll bill you for that smashed window, Rutherford."

I walked back to the car then, and drove away from Gunsmoke Acres.

It was almost closing time when I got back to the office. I don't know why I went there, except that I wanted something to do. Work is a good cure-all, and I still wasn't over Cam's death. I felt vastly reassured since my talk with Di Luca, and I was certain he'd find the killer. But finding the killer would not bring Cam back, and that was a difficult idea to get used to.

There was no going back. The memory could be nothing more than a memory now.

It was like hearing a song on the radio and not knowing the title of the tune. You wait for the disc jockey to repeat the title after the song has ended. But he goes into a commercial and then plays another record, and you never learn the title of the first song. You're left with only a haunting melody, in your mind, and nothing more. You can't go out to buy the record. You can't hear it again, except by chance.

Cam was that way. A song I'd heard. A lovely melody that had meant a lot. I hadn't learned more about it. And soon the melody would fade, and perhaps I'd hear it again sometime, by chance, sometime.

I guess my face showed what I was thinking. Jeanette looked up at me, and the smile dropped from her features.

"Hello, Mr. Blake," she said.

"Any calls?" I asked dully.

"Yes, Mr. Donato has been calling ever since you left. He seemed very angry, Mr. Blake."

"The hell with him," I said. "Anything else?"

"I'll make a list, if you like."

"Please. I'll be in my office."

I crossed the reception room and went into my own office and then I sat behind my desk and looked at Stagg Bellow's letter where I'd left it. I read it over, and it didn't strike me funny this time.

Jeanette came in with a list of calls, and I scanned it quickly. Donato had called five times since I'd left the office.

"You'd better get this joker for me, Jeanette," I said. Then, because I still wanted to do something, I said, "Never mind, I'll call myself. Let me have the number, will you?"

Jeanette brought me the number, and I dialed it rapidly. I didn't think the guy had much on his mind, but I didn't like to make an enemy where I could make a friend, and five calls warranted a return call.

I listened to the phone ringing on the other end, and then a sweet feminine voice said, "Universal Photostats, good afternoon."

"Mr. Donato, please," I said.

"Yes, sir. One moment, please."

I waited, remembering something about Donato now. He'd called the morning I'd found Del dead. He'd said something about...

"Hello." The voice was deep, and I pictured a big man with a lot of hair on his chest.

"Mr. Donato?"

"Yes."

"Mr. Blake of Gilbert and Blake."

"Well, Jesus, it's about time."

"Sorry I wasn't in to take your previous calls, Mr. Donato. This place has been in something of a turmoil."

Donato laughed loudly, a booming, hearty laugh, "You certainly must be busy. I wouldn't have kept calling, but I thought you were in a rush. I mean your partner…"

"Maybe you'd better fill me in, Mr. Donato. I'm afraid I don't know what this is all about."

"No? Oh, well sure. No trouble at all. We're an all-night place, you see. We do printing, too, and a lot of photographic work. Legal work, too. We don't get many orders at night, but there's always some men here working on a job."

"I see."

"Yeah, we got two shifts. You understand."

"Yes, I understand."

"Well, I was on the night shift a couple of nights back…let me see…it was Sunday night. Well, really Monday morning. Very early, you know. It was still dark. Before the morning shift came on."

"Yes."

"Well, Mr. Gilbert called, and he seemed in a very big rush. He said he needed some work done in a hurry, and could we do it for him."

"Mr. Gilbert called?" I asked. "Sunday night?"

"Well, Monday morning it was. Like I told you."

"Yes, yes, go on."

"So I said, sure. We can do it. We do a lot of rush jobs, you know. I told him we'd have them ready in a few hours."

"Have what ready?"

"Some photostats. He wanted a dozen made. He said I should take very good care of the original. Naturally, we always take good care…"

"Did he come down with the original?"

"No. I sent one of the men up. It's right around the corner."

"Was Mr. Gilbert alone when your man got here?"

"Yes. Yes, I think so. That's right. He went to the safe, the man told me, and got out this paper and told him to be very careful with it. Twelve copies, he wanted."

"Mr. Gilbert took the paper out of the safe?"

"Yeah. He got a folder out of the safe, brought it to his desk, and then took the paper from it. That's what my man told me."

"And…"

"Well, I called Monday to say the photostats were ready. I spoke to you, I think. You said you'd send a kid down for them, and he never came. We did a nice job, Mr. Blake, and since Mr. Gilbert seemed in a hurry, I've been calling you. I thought…"

"This photostat," I said. "Would you read it to me?"

"Sure, just a second."

I knew, of course. I knew, and, Di Luca had been right all along.

"Hello."

"Yes, I'm here."

"Here it is," Donato said. "I'll read it to you."

"Go ahead."

"*Gentlemen,*" he read. "*Thank you for your recent letter. This will grant you permission to handle exclusively the radio and television rights to all the published…*"

"That's enough," I said. "Thanks."

"Not at all. It's important, huh?" Donato asked.

"Not anymore," I said. "Not anymore."

13.

So there it was.

Another red herring.

And the agreement had really had nothing to do with it all along. Nothing at all. Del had sent the original to be photostated, and it wasn't difficult to figure why. He'd talked with Cam Stewart, and she'd told him she didn't remember a damned thing about signing any agreement. He'd come back to the city, realizing we were in for trouble if she stuck to that story. Instead of going directly home, or instead of going to Lydia's place or wherever he'd have preferred going, he'd gone directly to the office and taken care of getting more copies of that agreement made.

And he'd probably been killed shortly after Donato's man left with the agreement. The safe was still open, and the desk light was still burning.

I tried to recall the way I'd found him.

He was lying in front of the safe, and the contents of the Important Papers folder were scattered on the floor. That made sense, too. He'd probably gone back to the safe to lock the folder in again. That was when he'd been shot from the door.

So who?

Who knew he'd be at the office?

Someone who'd obviously followed him to Connecticut and back.

Well, who knew he was in Connecticut? Who knew he was with Cam Stewart? Who...

I remembered something. I remembered something, and I

knew suddenly who the murderer was. I swung out from behind the desk and left the office fast. Very fast.

I drove as rapidly as I could. It was close to five, and I met a
lot of home-bound traffic. I tried to keep patient, thinking of
the killer, and knowing what had rekindled the spark that led
to Cam's death. I blamed myself, and there was a deep feeling
of guilt inside me. But there was also a hatred that was slow
boiling, like a dark brew reaching up into my brain. I kept my
hands tight on the wheel, and my eyes glued to the road, and I
thanked the power of the big Buick, and I kept thinking of the
killer, and the hatred kept rising inside me.

I pulled up to the house, and I sprinted to the front door and
rang. The door opened a crack, and then opened wider.

"Josh! This is a surprise."

"I'll bet."

I walked into the room, and I spotted the suitcase right off,
with the underwear stacked beside it. I turned and said, "You
going somewhere, Gail?"

Gail Gilbert smiled. "Yes. A little trip, I thought. This confusion has been too much for me, Josh. I thought…"

"The spark's dead, huh? You've had a little time to pull yourself together, and you've read the writing on the wall. It's time
to blow."

"What the devil are you ranting about?" she asked, a per-
plexed frown crossing her forehead.

"Murder, Gail," I said. "Plain, simple motivated murder."

She stood with her shoulders back, her breasts tight and high
against the silk dress she wore. Her hair still looked wind-blown—
that carefully coiffed, wind-blown look. Her eyes were bright and
blue, with white flecks sharp against the pupils.

"All right," she said, "let's play games if you want to. I hope
you don't mind if I finish packing."

"Not at all. Pack a lot. It's going to be a long trip."

She cocked one raven brow in exasperation and then walked over to the suitcase, exaggerating the swing of her hips, still trying, even though it was all over now. She began putting the underwear into the valise. She arranged it in neat piles, carefully patting each pile. When she was finished with the underwear, she turned and went into the bedroom, coming back with a stack of sweaters.

"You're quiet," she said. "Maybe you're finished."

"I haven't started yet, Gail."

"Then start. Start and get it over with."

"All right, from the beginning. From when you first found out Del was playing house with Lydia, whenever that was. From when you learned he was the kind of husband people whisper about behind their hands. From when you first learned that, Gail."

"I've known that for a long time, Josh. If you're trying to build a murder story on…"

"Sure, it takes a while for the hatred to really build up. How long was it eating away inside you, Gail?"

"I don't see any reason to…"

"It reached the danger point last Friday. Del told you he was going to Connecticut to see a client. You didn't believe him. You followed him there, suspicious as hell, and your suspicions seemed correct. He *had* gone to see a woman. You followed him back to the office on Sunday night, and you killed him there."

"Don't be ridic…"

"You killed him, Gail. You killed him because the hatred and the jealousy were building in your heart for a long, long time. This was the last straw. This was the last lie, and you had a lonely weekend in Connecticut—while Del was with another woman—to think about it. And the hatred flamed higher, so you followed him, and you purged the hatred by filling his head with bullets. You killed him, Gail. You killed him while he stood near the safe, ready to…"

"All right, all right. I killed him. I killed the bastard and I'd do it again. I'd do it again right now. You understand that, Josh? I'd kill him again."

"But he wasn't enough, was he? The hatred wasn't quite purged, and so you went after Lydia, and you gave her the same thing he got, and that would have been the end of it but…"

"Was it wrong? Was it wrong to kill the slut who'd taken him away from me?" She glared at me, and then her mouth twisted into an ugly thing. "Sure, I killed her. I killed her before she even had a chance to scream. I waited for her, and I gave it to her, and I watched the goddamn whore while she died!"

I looked into her eyes, behind her eyes, and I saw the whole tortured world that was Gail Gilbert's. I was going to tell her that I knew she was the one who'd fired at me from the roof across from my apartment. I was going to tell her that she'd tried to kill me because even I had turned away her love. And failing in that, and with a new hatred kindled within her, she had gone to Connecticut and killed Cam Stewart—killed the last woman Del had been with. I was going to tell her all that, but the look in her eyes stopped me, and I held my tongue.

"What's wrong with me?" she asked. "What is it, Josh? Why did he turn to her? Why, why?"

"I don't know, Gail."

"I'm pretty," she said, almost to herself. "You know that I…I'm warm…and pretty…" She caught herself and stopped, and a crafty glint came into her eyes. She seemed to remember suddenly that I knew she'd killed her husband and the two women. She reached into the suitcase, and the .45 that came up in her fist was big and black and ugly.

"How'd you find out, Josh? How?"

"One slip, Gail. I don't think you were trying very hard to cover. I don't think people do when they're murdering whole-sale."

"What slip? What?"

"The morning Del was killed. I went home when the police were through with me, and I found you there. You were looped, and you insisted Del had been with a woman the night before. I told you he'd been with a client. You said, *'No, Josh, A woman. I know.'* That's what you said, Gail. I remembered that a little while ago in my office, and it was all clear then. You see, neither Del nor I knew that Cam Stewart was a woman. It's no secret, but there just aren't many people who know. You knew because you'd seen her. You followed Del there, and you followed him back and…"

"Shut up," she said suddenly. She lifted the .45, and I knew she'd used it three times before, and when I saw her thumb snap off the safety, I knew she could use it again.

"Don't be foolish, Gail," I said.

She didn't answer me. She kept staring at me with her chest heaving, and her finger around the trigger, her knuckles white.

"You'd be very foolish, Gail," I repeated. "He's dead now. He's dead and gone, and I'm not the sucker I used to be."

She looked at me quizzically, and she said nothing. I was beginning to sweat, but she couldn't see the sweat. She saw only the smile on my face, and the phony lust in my eyes—the lust that covered the fear inside me.

"I thought a long time, Gail. I wondered what he'd have done in my place. With me dead, and with my wife in his arms. Lovely. Desirable. Everything a man could want. I wondered what he would have done, and I know now, Gail. I know damn well." I took a step closer to her, watching the gun, wetting my lips and hoping she was taking the hook. Because if she wasn't, there'd be one more corpse, and the tag on his toe would say Joshua Blake.

"You…you mean that, Josh?" she asked. She still held the gun pointed at my stomach. But she wanted to believe. She wanted desperately to believe me.

"Honey," I said, "I'm through being a sucker. This should have happened a long time ago. It should have happened when you came to my apartment, only I was too much of a fool to see then. And it should have happened here yesterday. It didn't, but it's not too late. It's not too late, Gail."

I took another step closer, and I held out my arms and she stared at me for a moment, her face trembling. I saw the .45 waver, and when I looked into her eyes, all the loneliness was there, all the hunger of a desirable woman who's been kicked around for a long time, all the emptiness and the yearning. For a second, I felt like a Grade-A heel. And then I remembered Cam Stewart, and I didn't feel anything anymore.

Gail lowered the gun. She lowered it, and she came to me, and she lifted her head and her lips, and there was gratitude in her eyes and something else, something that comes only when you know you're loved and wanted.

I hit her. I hit her hard with my balled fist, right on the point of her jaw. I felt like a bastard because I'd never hit a woman in my life. Her eyes went blank instantly, and she dropped to the floor with the .45 clunking heavily beside her. I looked down at her, with her dress up over her thighs, her mouth open, her eyes shut, the long black lashes against her face, and I wondered what had driven Del.

I felt tired all at once, very tired.

I went to the phone and dialed Di Luca. I told him I had his murderer, and I told him where I was.

He made it to Yonkers in fifteen minutes flat.

✽

I got roaring drunk that night. I went to a bar called The Cock-atoo, and I tried to wash it all out of my mind. I drank heavily and steadily, and after a while the memories began to fade. I didn't think they'd ever leave completely. But for a little while, I was free. Just for a little while.

I sat at the bar, and I drank, and I listened to the muted music of the juke, and I watched the soft lighting under the mirror.

The blonde appeared magically in the mirror.

"Hello, Josh," she said.

I turned to face her stool, and our knees touched, and the touch was familiar. I looked at her, and I didn't remember. There was a puzzled smile on her face. She kept smiling at me, and I put my hand on her knee and said, "Baby, you and I should…"

"I know," she said.

"You know?"

She smiled again, and I remembered all at once. She closed her hand over mine and whispered, "My name is Janice. This is where I came in."

WANT MORE
McBAIN?

**Read on for a
long-lost novelette by
ED McBAIN
featuring MATT CORDELL,
the disgraced detective from
THE GUTTER AND THE GRAVE.**

**And for another exciting
novel-length crime story, try
SO NUDE, SO DEAD and
THE GUTTER AND THE GRAVE,
both available now from your favorite
local or online bookseller!**

Now Die in It

He woke me by shaking me and shouting my name, and I came out of sleep with a cocked fist, ready to smash his head open. The nightmare had been on me again, the dream in which Toni laughed at me, half-naked in Parker's arms, the dream that always ended the same way: my .45 going back and down, again and again, against Parker's rotten face, and Toni screaming over and over in the background. Only this time there was a new voice in the dream, and it shouted, "Matt! Matt Cordell!"

I jerked up violently, and I brought my fist back, and I felt strong hands close on my wrist.

"Matt, for God's sake, it's me, Rudy!"

I forced my eyes open and blinked in the semidarkness of the room. There was a cot under me, and a blanket over me, and a gorilla sat on the edge of the cot, leaning over me. The gorilla's name was Rudy, and I remembered him vaguely as a guy I'd know long ago, a guy who lived somewhere in the Bronx.

I passed my hand over my face, trying to wipe away the sleep. I rubbed my bristled jaw, then I reached for the pint of wine, took a long swallow, and asked, "What the hell is it, Rudy?"

"Boy, you're harder to find than a needle in a haystack."

"Maybe you haven't been trying the right places." We were in a two-bits-a-night flophouse on the Bowery, and I didn't imagine Rudy was well acquainted with this particular type of resort. "What's so important, Rudy?"

"We need your help, Matt. My wife told me to get a detective."

"Then why don't you get one? Is that why you woke me? Rudy, I ought to…"

"Matt, you're the only one I know. I came because you're the only one I know."

"Don't you read the papers, you stupid bastard?" I said. "I don't own a license anymore. The cops took it away when I beat up the guy I found with my wife. Now get the hell out and…"

"It's my wife's sister, Matt," he said, ignoring me. "The reason I came is she's pregnant."

"Good for her," I said.

"You don't follow, Matt. She's a seventeen-year-old kid. Been living with us since my father-in-law passed away. She ain't married, Matt."

"So? For Christ's sake, Rudy, what the hell do you want me to do about it?"

"My wife wants to find the guy who done it. Matt, she's been driving me nuts. The kid won't tell her, and she's beginning to swell up like a balloon. My wife wants to find him to make him do the right thing."

"What's her name?"

"My sister-in-law's?"

"Yeah."

"Betty."

"And she won't tell you the guy's name?"

"No, Matt. She's got a funny sense of loyalty or something, I guess. My wife's been after her ever since she found out about it, but she won't peep."

"What makes you think I can find the guy?"

"If anyone can, you can, Matt."

I shook my head. "Rudy, do me a favor. Go to a certified agency, will you? Get yourself a detective who can stand up straight."

"I'll tell you the truth, Matt. I can't afford it. I got a kid of my own, a lot of mouths to feed. Help me, Matt, will you?"

"No! God damn it, I don't practice anymore. Go back home, Rudy. Forget you found me. Do that, will you?"

"It ain't so much for me, Matt. It's the wife. This thing is making a wreck of her. Matt, I never asked you for anything before, but this is something else. Believe me, if I didn't have to ask you…"

"All right, all right!" I shouted. I cursed and swung my legs over the side of the cot, reaching for my shoes on the floor. They were cold, and I cursed a little more. When I finally had them laced, I asked, "You still a night watchman?"

"Yes," Rudy said.

"You got a car with you?"

"Yes, Matt." He looked at me hopefully. "Are you going to help me?"

"Yeah, yeah. I'm going to help. I'm the craziest bastard alive, but I'll help you. Let's go," I said.

His car was parked downstairs. He drove quickly and he filled me in on a few more details as we headed for the Bronx. His wife Madeline had found out Betty was pregnant about a month ago. The kid was already four months gone by that time, and Madeline was frantic. Both she and Rudy talked to the girl, but they couldn't get anything out of her. They asked discreet questions around the neighborhood, but since they didn't want the secret to get out, they had to be very careful—and their questioning had netted a big fat zero. They'd asked the kid to get rid of the baby, and she'd refused. And then they'd asked her to have it at a home where they'd take the baby off her hands as soon as it was born, and that drew a blank also. All the while, Betty refused to name the guy.

"That's a little strange, isn't it?" I asked Rudy.

"Sure," Rudy agreed. "But you know how these teenagers are. Crazier'n hell."

"Is she pretty?"

"Beautiful," Rudy said. "Blue eyes, black hair. Looks just the way my wife did when she was that age. You ever meet Madeline, Matt?"

"No."

"Well, she's changed a lot since I first married her. But the kid is a dead ringer for what she used to look like. You'll see."

"Does she have a lot of boy friends?"

"The usual. Neighborhood kids mostly."

"Did you talk to any of them?"

"A few. I couldn't tell them what I was after, though, so it was kind of tough."

"Whal kind of a crowd was she in? Fast?"

"I really don't know, Matt. She didn't talk about it."

"Uh-huh."

"You think you'll find the guy?"

"You haven't given me a hell of a lot to go on."

"That's all there is, Matt. Maybe Madeline can give you a little more. She talked to her more than I did."

"We'll see," I said.

He pulled the car up in front of an apartment house in the East Bronx. A few women were sitting on chairs in front of the house, and when Rudy got out of the car, they nodded at him. When I got out, they stared at me distastefully, and then went back to their gossip.

We climbed four flights and then Rudy knocked on a painted brown door. The door opened wide, and a woman's voice reached us.

"What took you so long?" it said. The voice belonged to a woman of about twenty-eight, a few years younger than both Rudy and me. Her black hair was pulled to the back of her neck, tied there with a white ribbon. Her eyes were tired, very tired.

"Gee, honey," Rudy said, "I made it as fast as I could."

"You didn't make it fast enough," Madeline said tonelessly. "Betty's dead."

❦

I was standing behind Rudy, so I couldn't see his face. He backed up a few paces, though, and I could imagine what was on his face.

"D-d-dead?" he stammered. "Betty? Dead?"

It was silent in the hall for the space of a heart tick, and then I followed him into the apartment. The furniture was old, but the place was neat and well kept.

Rudy buried his face in his hands. Madeline sat in a chair opposite him; there were no tears on her face.

"Was it a suicide?" I asked her.

"No," she said. "The police called about ten minutes ago. They found her in Yonkers. She…she was strangled, they said."

Rudy suddenly raised his head.

"This is Matt Cordell, Madeline. Matt, this is my wife."

She mumbled, "How do you do?" and I nodded. Then a silence invaded the room. Madeline looked at me for a long time, and finally said, "I still want you to find him, Mr. Cordell."

"Well, the police will probably…"

"I want *you* to find him. I want you to find him and beat him black and blue, and then you can turn him over to the police. I'll pay you, Mr. Cordell." She stood up abruptly and walked into the kitchen. I heard her moving things on the pantry shelf. When she came back, she was holding a wad of bills in her hand.

"We were saving this for a new car," she said. "I'll give it to you. All of it. Just find the one who did this to Betty. Just find him and make him sorry. Cripple him if you have to. Find him, Mr. Cordell." She paused and thrust the bills at me. "Here."

"Keep the money," I said. "I'll look for him, but if I find him, he goes straight to the police."

Her lower lip began to tremble, and then the tears started, the tears she'd been holding in check for a long time now. I walked into the hallway with Rudy, and I whispered, "Where'd she hang out? Who were some of those guys you questioned?"

"There's an ice-cream parlor off Burke Avenue. Lots of them in that neighborhood. This one is called The Dewdrop. You know the kind of place. Bunch of teenage kids hang out there. She used to go to this one a lot, I think."

"Rough crowd?"

"I don't think so. Here, I'll give you the address." He fished in his wallet and came up with a scrap of paper. A bunch of numbers and a street name were scrawled on the paper with a ballpoint pen. I read the address, looked at it until I had memorized it. Rudy put it back into his wallet. "They seemed like nice kids, Matt."

"Yeah," I said. "It takes a real nice kid to choke a girl."

"Let me know how you make out, Matt."

"I will, Rudy. You'd better go back to your wife."

I started looking for the address Rudy had given me. It turned out to be a small, narrow shop set between two buildings in a space which would have made a better tailor shop—where all the work is done backstage—than an ice-cream parlor. But ice-cream parlor it was. There was no question about it. The words *The Dewdrop* had been painted onto the plate-glass window, and the same artist had painted the picture of an ice-cream scoop dripping a great big blob of ice cream. The art work was amateurish. It gave the place an uncertain look; it was, possibly, that very look which appealed to the teenagers. I opened the door, and a bell tinkled, and then the bell was drowned in the roar from the jukebox, and I wished I had a drink.

There was a counter with stools on the right-hand side of the store, and four booths painted red, blue, yellow and green on the left-hand side. A man with a mustache was working behind the counter. Two teenage boys were sitting in the booth farthest from the door, beating their feet against the floor in time with the music. The jukebox was emitting the high wail of someone in his death throes, the piano and guitar behind him plinkety-plunking in a monotonous funeral-march tempo. I walked to the counter.

"You the owner?" I asked.

The guy with the mustache was scooping nuts from cans into his fancy sundae jars. "Yeah," he said. "Why?"

"I'm trying to find out about a girl named Betty," I said.

"Betty who?"

I dug in my memory for the name Rudy had given me on the ride up to the Bronx. "Betty Richards," I said. "Do you know her?"

"I get a lot of kids in here," the man said, carefully scooping the nuts and redepositing them. "Ask them kids in the booth. They'll know better than me."

"Thanks," I said. I went over to the booth. The boys didn't look up at me. They kept tapping their feet and listening to the juke.

At last, one of them raised his head. He was about eighteen, the sure look of adolescence on his face, the knowledgeable look of a man of the world. He turned to his buddy. "Brother, can you spare a dime?" he said.

His buddy stopped stomping his feet for a moment. He glanced at me. "No handouts today, Mac," he said. "Drift along. The park's thataway."

"I'm a friend of Betty's," I said.

"Betty who?"

"Richards."

"So?" the first kid said. "What about her?"

"That's what I wanted to ask."

"I don't know her," the first kid said.

The second kid got up, went to the juke, made another selection, then came back to the booth. As if he hadn't already spoken to me, he said to his friend, "Who's this, Bob?"

"He's looking for Betty Richards," Bob said.

"Yeah?" He studied me, as if he were debating whether or not to throw me out of the store. I was half-hoping he'd try it.

"Not exactly looking for her," I said. "I want to know a few things about her."

"Yeah? What kind of things?"

"What's your name, junior?"

"Who wants to know?"

"I do. Matt Cordell."

"Yeah?"

"Yeah."

We held a staring contest for about two minutes while the boy sized me up and made his decision.

"Jack," he said at last.

"Do we talk about Betty now?"

"I ain't her brother," Jack said.

"What do you know about her?"

"What do you want to know?"

"Who she dated," I said. "When she came in here. Who she hung around with when she was here. Things like that."

"Why do you want to know?"

I was getting tired of playing footsie, so I said, "Because someone strangled her a little while ago. She's dead."

Bob's feet stopped jiggling. Jack stared at me.

"Yeah?" he said.

"Yeah."

"We don't know nothing about it," he said.

"Nobody said you did. Tell me about Betty."

"She used to come in here, but she never stayed long. She'd come in, have a Coke, and then take off."

"You sure, Jack?"

"I'm positive. Ain't that right, Bob?"

The other kid nodded. "That's right, mister. She just came and went, that's all."

"She date any of the kids who come in here?"

"Nope. Most of the guys have steadies. They wouldn't ask for trouble."

"Did she ever come in here with anyone?"

"A guy, you mean?"

"Yes."

Jack thought this over for a moment. "No. Never. She'd just come in, hang around a while, and then leave. Just like I told you."

"Did she ever say she had to meet anyone after she left?"

"No, not to me. She wouldn't tell something like that to a guy. Maybe she told one of the girls, I don't know."

"She friendly with any of the girls who come in here?"

"I guess not," Jack said. "She was pretty much a lone wolf, Betty was."

"How about Donna?" Bob asked.

"Oh, yeah. Donna," Jack said.

"Who's Donna?" I asked.

"The girl who works here nights. A waitress. She's real sharp. An older girl. She's real sharp, ain't she, Bob?"

"Yeah," Bob said. "She's the most."

"How old is she?"

"Twenty-three, twenty-four. Yeah, about that. Wouldn't you say about that, Bob?"

"Yeah, about that," Bob agreed.

"She was kind of friendly with Betty," Jack said.

"Where can I reach her?"

"I like Donna," Jack said. "You can find her for yourself. I don't know nothing."

"Look…"

"She's a nice girl. I don't want to get her in no trouble."

"Where do I find her?"

"That's your problem."

"Sonny," I said, "maybe you didn't understand me. Betty was killed. Murdered. Finding her murderer is a little more important than protecting the pure white innocence of Donna."

"She ain't so pure," Bob said.

"She ain't so innocent, either," Jack said.

"She's sharp," Bob said.

"The most," Jack said.

"And she was friendly with Betty, right?" I asked.

"Yeah. Well, they talked. Whenever Betty came in, they'd talk."

"About what?"

"I don't know," Jack said.

"Donna knows," I told him. "What's her address?"

We held another short staring contest. I won again. Jack sighed.

"All right, all right," he said. "She lives right around the corner." He took a pencil stub from his pocket and then pulled a napkin from the container on the table. "Donna Crane," he said, writing the name on the napkin. Under that, he wrote the address, and then said, "It's the yellow apartment house on the corner. Apartment 3-C. You can't miss it."

"Thanks," I said.

"You'll have your hands full with her," Bob warned me. "She's sharp."

"I know," I said. "The most."

And I left them.

The card under the buzzer read *Donna Crane.* I pushed the buzzer and walked to the lobby door, then waited. Nothing happened, so I pushed the buzzer again, waited a few more minutes, and then pressed two buzzers at random, hoping one of them would be home. The door clicked open, and I started up the steps to the third floor. It was a nice apartment house, lower-middle class, with no hallway smells and no broken plaster. The floors were clean, and even the windows on each landing were freshly washed. I pulled up alongside 3-C and twisted the old-fashioned screw-type bell in the door. It rattled loudly, and when I'd waited for three minutes with no results, I twisted it again.

"Shake it, don't break it," a girl's voice said.

I waited until I heard footsteps approaching the door, and then I passed my hand over my hair in an abortive attempt to make myself look a little more presentable.

The door swung wide, and the girl looked out at me curiously.

"Christ," she said, "did you get his number?"

"Whose number?" I asked.

"The guy who ran you over," she said.

"Very funny," I said. "You Donna Crane?"

"The same. If you're selling something, you need a shave."

"You knew Betty Richards," I said.

"Sure." Her eyes narrowed, and she said, "Hey, you're not… no, you couldn't be."

"Who?"

"Never mind. You coming in?" She grinned coyly. "The neighbors will talk."

She was blonde, blonde the way Toni had been. She wore a green sweater that had been knitted around her and black shorts turned up far enough to exhibit the graceful curve of her thigh. Orchard Beach had provided her with a Bronx tan, but it didn't hide the sophistication of her face. She was Broadway on Burke Avenue, with all the glitter and all the tinsel—and I guess maybe the neighbors did talk a little about her.

"Are you or aren't you coming in, pal?" she prompted.

I stepped into the apartment, and she closed the door behind me. The blinds were still drawn, and the place had all the dim coolness of Grant's Tomb. I smelled coffee brewing in the kitchen as she led me into the living room.

She sat opposite me and folded her long, tanned legs under her with practiced ease. She propped one elbow on the sofa back, tilted her head and asked, "So now, what about Betty?"

"Just like that, huh? Don't care who I am, or anything."

"I know who you are."

"Oh."

"Sure. I read the papers. I saw the pictures. Matt. Matt…" She searched her memory. "Take off the beard and some of the whiskey flab, and add Cordell to the Matt. The screwed shamus." I didn't answer, so she said, "I'm right, aren't I?"

"You're right," I said wearily.

"I thought they threw you in the jug or something."

"They dropped charges."

"Yeah, that's right," she said, nodding. "I remember now. The babe went to Mexico, didn't she?"

"Can it," I said.

Her eyes opened wide, and she thrust out her lower lip. "Didn't know you were still warm for her form, pal."

"I said can it!"

She shrugged, and her breasts bobbed beneath the tight sweater. "Son, if you don't like this brand of jive, you know where you can go, don't you?"

I stood up. "Listen…" I started to say, but I couldn't stop her.

"Nobody told you to marry a slut. You picked a dud, and you…"

I slapped her with my open hand, catching her on the side of her jaw. Her head reeled back, and she scrambled off the couch, her eyes slitted. "Get the hell out of here," she said.

"Not until I ask a few questions."

"You got no right to ask questions. The cops took your license, pal."

"What did you and Betty talk about?" I asked.

Abruptly, she started to walk toward the phone. I grabbed her wrist and swung her around, and she came up against me, hard, her face inches from mine. She was rearing her head back to spit when I clamped my hand over her mouth. She wriggled, freed her mouth, and then bit down on my hand, her upper and lower teeth almost meeting in my flesh. I shoved her away from me, and she ran back at me, throwing herself at me like a wildcat. But there was something more than anger in her eyes this time, something I recognized instantly.

This time I grabbed her arm and twisted it behind her, and when she brought her head back, my lips came down against hers. She struggled for a moment, and then went limp in my arms. I lifted her and carried her to the sofa, her lips buried in my neck, her hands running over my back. I smelled coffee from the kitchen, and then there was only the smell of her hair and her body in my nostrils, and the sound of her ragged breathing in the cool, dim living room.

She was curled up like a contented cat, a cigarette glowing in her hand, relaxed against the cushions of the sofa. There was a pleased smile on her face, and some of the hardness had rubbed off to leave features that were young and nicely boned.

"You need a shave," she said.

"I know." I lit a cigarette, blew out a stream of smoke and asked, "Do we talk now?"

She closed her eyes briefly, still smiling. "Must we?"

"We must."

"Then talk, Matt."

"What did Betty have to say to you?"

"Why?"

"Because she's dead. Because someone was careless enough to strangle her."

"Oh," she said. That was all. Just a small "oh" but her face had grown pale beneath its tan, and she was breathing harder.

"You *did* talk? You and Betty?"

"Yes. Yes, we talked sometimes."

"What about?"

"Dead," she said. She tasted the word, and then repeated it. "Dead. A nice kid, too. Mixed up, but nice."

"Mixed up about what?"

"What are most seventeen-year-old kids mixed up about? Love. Sex." She shrugged. "The same thing."

"Not always. How was she mixed up?"

"This guy…"

"What guy?" I asked quickly.

"A guy she was going with. She'd sit and talk about him when she came to the shop. She had it bad, all right."

"What was his name?"

"Freddie. That's what she called him. Freddie."

"Freddie what?"

"She never said. Just Freddie."

"Great. What did she say about him?"

"The usual. You know."

"I don't know."

Donna eyed me levelly. "You can be an irritating louse, you know?"

"Sure," I said. "Tell me what she told you about him."

"Well, she didn't want her family to know about him, for some reason. She used to meet him on the sneak. She'd come in to the Dewdrop as a blind, stay there a while, and then take off. She usually met him at about ten or so, I think."

"Did she tell you that?"

"Well, no. But she always left the place at about that time. I figured…"

"Where'd she go when she left?"

"I never went with her."

"Did she tell you how she first happened to meet this guy? Where? When?"

"No."

"Did she ever mention his age?"

"No."

"What he did for a living?"

"No."

I ran a hand over my face. "That helps a lot." I sat there for a few seconds and then asked, "Anything to drink besides coffee here?"

"Coffee! Holy Jesus!" She untangled her tanned legs and ran across the room, and I watched, knowing there was nothing but her under that sweater. I watched her go, noticing the curve of her legs, and the firmness of her body, and then she was in the kitchen turning down the gas under the pot.

"Beer all right?" she asked.

"It'll do."

"This isn't Joe's Grill, pal," she said. I heard the refrigerator door open, and then heard the sound of a bottle being placed on the kitchen table. There were a few more kitchen sounds, and then the fizz of the beer as she took off the cap. When she came into the living room, she was carrying the bottle in one hand and a steaming cup of coffee balanced in the other hand.

She gave me the bottle and said, "If you want a glass, go get it. I've only got three hands."

"This'll be fine."

She curled up again, and I took a deep drag of the bottle

while she sipped at the hot coffee, peering at me over the edge of the cup.

"Did she ever describe this Freddie?" I asked. I wiped my lips and held the bottle in my lap.

"Nope. I gathered he was from Squaresville, though."

"What makes you say that?"

"The questions she asked. A hip character wouldn't leave questions like that in a kid's head."

"What kind of questions?"

"Well, personal things."

"Like what? Honey, I'm not a dentist. Let's have less teeth-pulling."

"Don't get it in an uproar, buster," she told me. She took an angry gulp of coffee, burning her tongue and shooting me a hot glare.

"She asked me how to…well, you know." She paused, waiting for my comment. When I made none, she added, "You know."

"In short," I said, "you think she was pretty innocent?"

"Innocent? Brother, she was the original fiddler who didn't know his bass from his oboe."

"Well," I said, "somebody taught her damned fast."

"How do you mean?"

"She was pregnant when she was killed."

"Ouch!" Donna Crane winced and then shook her head slowly. She uncrossed her legs. "You think this Freddie…"

"Could be."

She put her coffee cup down and said, "I wish you luck. If he did it, I hope you get him."

I walked into the foyer and paused with my hand on the doorknob. She reached up to touch my face and asked, "Do you ever shave?"

"Sometimes. Why?"

She shrugged, and her chest did things again. Then her lips were on mine, gently this time. My hands found the small of her back, and she pressed closer to me for an instant, drawing away almost immediately. "Take a shave sometime, Matt. And then come back."

I opened the door and stepped into the comparatively bright hallway, grinning back at her. "Maybe I will, Donna. Maybe I will."

Freddie.

Just a name. Just one Freddie out of thousands of Freddies in the city, the millions of Freddies in the world. Gather them all together, and then pick a Freddie out of the bunch.

There was a mild breeze on the air, and it searched my face and the open throat of my shirt. The streets were crowded with people seduced by spring. They breathed deeply of her fragrance, flirted back at her, treated her as the mistress she was, the wanton who would grow old with summer's heat and die with autumn's first chill blast. The man with his hot-dog cart stood in the gutter, and the sun-seekers crowded the sauerkraut pot, thronged the umbrella-topped stand. The high-school girls ambled home with all the time in the world, with all their lives ahead of them. The men stood around the candy stores and the delicatessens talking about the fights or the coming baseball season, and they looked at silk-stockinged legs and wished for a stronger breeze.

Or they went about their jobs, delivering mail, washing windows, fixing cars, and they drew in deeply of the warm air and sighed a little. It was spring, at last. And one of them was Freddie.

I walked along Burke Avenue, wondering how long it had been since I'd eaten a hot dog, since I'd seen a baseball game.

A long time. A long, long time. And how long ago to seventeen? How many years, how many centuries?

What's a seventeen-year-old kid like? No longer the girl, not yet the woman— Why does a seventeen-year-old hide a lover? Love at seventeen is a wonderland of dreamy records and beach parties and tender kisses and silent handclasps. It is not a thing to hide.

But Betty Richards hid her love, and her love was hidden behind the name of Freddie, and New York City is a big place.

I needed a drink. I needed one because I couldn't think straight anymore. I was ready to go to Rudy and say, "Pal, I'm lost. Me and eight million others all have spring fever, only it shows more on me because I'm still in love with a bitch who done me wrong, like the song says, Rudy. So let's just drop it and forget it and let the cops do the work. Okay, Rudy? Okay, pal?"

But would a cop understand a kid with her first love? Would a cop give one good goddam?

I cursed myself, and I had my drink, and then I started from the beginning again, and the beginning was The Dewdrop.

I didn't go inside this time.

I stopped at the door, and then began retracing my steps. Betty Richards had walked out of this shop on many a night. Ten o'clock, and Freddie waiting. Where? I started up the street.

A car? Would he pick her up in a car? Maybe. But not here. If Betty had gone to all this trouble to hide the guy, he certainly wouldn't pick her up outside the ice-cream parlor. Not with a bunch of curious teenagers inside. A few blocks away then? Even that seemed like an unnecessary risk. A few miles away? A dozen miles away? Why not? But where?

I turned left and started walking toward Burke Avenue. The side street was lined with private houses. The front stoops sported fat women in housedresses who looked up when I passed and muttered about what the neighborhood was coming to. When I got to Burke Avenue, I looked right and left. A block down on my left, looking like a blackened monster against the sky, was the elevated structure. I turned and headed for it, walking past the dry-cleaning shop, the delicatessen, the bakery, pausing at the newsstand on the corner, and then noticing the hack stand. It was a hack stand for three cabs, right behind the newsstand which crouched under the steps leading to the elevated structure.

A cab was at the curb. A driver sat behind the wheel reading a comic book and picking at his teeth with a matchbook cover. I poked my head into the taxi.

"Hop in, mister," he said. "Where you going?" Then he got a good look at me. "Sure you can afford the ride, Mac?" he said.

"I'm not riding," I told him.

"I don't believe in staking strangers to drinks," he said. "So shove off."

"I'm not looking for a stake, either," I said.

"No? What then? You passing the time of day?"

"This your regular hack stand?"

"Sure."

"Ever been here around ten at night?"

"Lots of times. Why?"

"Ever carry a young girl, blue eyes, black hair. A very pretty young girl—about seventeen?"

"How the hell should I know? I carry lots of pretty…"

"This one might have taken a cab regularly. Or maybe she went up to the elevated. Remember seeing her?" I was guessing now, of course, and the guess might be a bit wide, but I figured any rendezvous Betty may have had was probably a thing with a set time and a set place. And Donna Crane had told me that Betty usually left the ice-cream parlor at ten.

"Why do you want to know, Mac?" the cabby said.

"I'm interested."

"You better take off before I call a cop."

"Look," I said, "this girl was killed. Her sister hired me to…"

"Jesus," he said. He squinched his eyes down tight, swallowed his Adam's apple and allowed it to bob up into his throat again. "Jesus."

"Do you remember her?"

"Blue eyes," he said. "Black hair. Seventeen."

"Yeah. If she took a cab, it would be at about ten. Did you ever carry her?"

The cabby shook his head. "Nope. I'd remember if I did. Why don't you ask some of the other guys? They pull in from time to time, whenever they ain't got a fare. Ask them. Maybe they'll remember."

"Thanks," I said. His was the only cab in the hack stand at the moment. I went upstairs to the train station and talked to the man in the change booth. He didn't remember Betty Richards, either. I sighed, went down to the street, and headed for Rudy's place.

It wasn't far from Burke Avenue, and I didn't mind the walk because it was such a nice day. I climbed the four flights and knocked on the painted brown door, and waited.

Rudy answered the door.

"Matt, come in, come in."

I walked into the apartment, looked around for Madeline, wondering if she'd gotten over the first shock of knowing her sister was dead. Rudy followed my glance and said, "She's in the bedroom. She's taking it kind of hard, Matt."

"You know any Freddie?" I asked.

"Who?"

"Freddie."

Rudy seemed to consider this for a moment. "No," he said slowly, "I don't think so. What's his last name?"

"All I've got is Freddie."

"Is it a lead, Matt? I mean, do you think this Freddie is the one who did it?"

"Maybe. You think Madeline would know him?"

"I don't know, Matt." He glanced at his watch hastily. "Gee, kid," he said, "I have to run. The day watchman goes off at five. I relieve him then, and I ain't relieved, myself, until one in the morning."

I looked at the clock on the kitchen wall. It was nearing four-thirty. "Will you get Madeline for me before you leave?"

"Sure. Just a minute."

He went into the bedroom, and I heard their muffled voices behind the closed door. It was very still in the living room. The sounds from the street climbed the brick facing of the building and sifted through the open windows. The breeze lifted the curtains silently. They hung on the air like restless specters, falling and rising again. The bedroom door opened, and Madeline came out with Rudy's arm around her shoulders. Her eyes were red-rimmed and her nose was raw from constant blowing.

"I have to run," Rudy said again. "I'll see you, Matt."

"Sure," I said.

He pecked Madeline on the cheek and then walked to the door and left.

Madeline moved to the window, stood there motionless looking down at the street below.

"Do you know a guy named Freddie?" I asked.

She didn't answer for a long time, and then she said, "What? I'm sorry, I didn't…"

"Freddie. Do you know anyone named Freddie? Did Betty have any friends by that name? Anybody?"

Madeline shook her head wearily. "No. No, I don't know any-one by that name. Why?"

I shrugged. "Nothing yet. Have you got a picture of Betty?"

"Yes. Someplace there's a picture."

"May I have it?"

"All right," she said dully. She left the room again, and I heard her rummaging around in the bedroom closet. The springs on the bed squeaked when she sat down. There were other sounds, leaves being turned, and then a gentle sobbing again. I heard her blow her nose, and I waited, and the clock on the kitchen wall threw minutes into the room. She came out at last, drying her eyes again, and handed me a small snapshot.

Rudy had been right. His sister-in-law was a beautiful kid with a clean-scrubbed look of freshness about her.

"I'll bring it back," I said.

"All right." She nodded, walked over to the window again and stared out. She was still looking down at the street when I left, closing the door gently behind me.

The cop was waiting for me just outside the building. I saw him there, started to step around him, almost bumped into him as he moved into my path.

I lifted my head, and our eyes locked. I didn't like what I saw.

"Excuse me," I said.

I started to go around him again when he clamped a big paw on my shoulder. "Just a second," he said.

I stopped, my eyes studying his face. He was a big guy, with a thin nose and pleasant blue eyes. He was smiling, and the smile wasn't pleasant. "What's the trouble, officer?" I asked.

"No trouble," he answered. "You Matt Cordell?"

A frown edged onto my forehead. "Yes. What…"

"Want to come along with me?" he asked pleasantly.

I kept staring at him. "Why? What do you want with me?"

"We've had a complaint, Cordell."

"What kind of a complaint?"

"They'll explain it to you."

"Suppose you explain it," I said.

"Suppose I don't," the cop answered.

"Look," I said, "don't blind me with your badge. I've had enough cops in my hair to last me…"

He grabbed the cuff of my jacket and twisted it in his fist, bringing my arm up behind me at the same time. I winced in pain, and the cop said, "Let's do it the easy way, Cordell. This is a nice quiet neighborhood."

"Sure," I said. "Just let go my goddamned arm."

He stopped twisting it, but he kept holding to the cuff, edging me toward the curb and the squad car I hadn't noticed until just then.

"Hop in," he said, holding open the door. "This one is on the city."

I got in and he climbed in behind me, wedging me between himself and the driver. He closed the door and said, "Okay, Sam." The cop behind the wheel threw the car into gear and shoved off.

We pulled up alongside a gray stone building with green lights hanging on either side of the door. The cop held the car door open for me, and then the driver stood on the sidewalk with his hand on the butt of his holstered .38 Police Special while the first cop and I climbed the steps to the precinct station.

The cop led me straight to the desk and said, "I've got Cordell, Ed. Want to tell the lieutenant?"

"Go on in," the cop behind the desk said. "Lieutenant's expecting you."

The big cop nodded, shoved me ahead of him down a hallway near the front of the station. He opened a door for me about halfway down the hall, gestured with his thumb and then added another shove to make sure I went the right way.

The plainclothes man sitting behind the desk stood up when I came in. He nodded at the cop and said, "All right, Jim. I'll take it from here." Jim saluted smartly, like a rookie after corporal's stripes, and then left me alone with the plainclothes man. A plaque read: *Detective-Lieutenant Gunnisson.*

"What's it all about, Lieutenant?" I asked.

Gunnisson was a smallish cop with a balding head and weary eyes. His mouth echoed the weariness by drooping loosely down to an almost invisible chin. He looked more like the caretaker in a museum than a police lieutenant. I wondered which Congressman his family had known.

"You're Matt Cordell, aren't you?"

"Yes."

"Got a complaint, Cordell."

"So I've heard."

He lifted his brows quickly, and his brown eyes snapped to my face. "Don't get snotty, Cordell. We're just itching to jug you."

"On what charge?"

"Practicing without a license."

"Where'd you dream that one up?"

"We got a complaint."

"Who from?"

"Phone call. Clocked at—" he glanced at a paper on his desk "—four forty-five."

"Who from?"

"Caller wouldn't give a name. Said you were investigating a case and thought we should look into it. What about it, Cordell?"

"It's all horse manure."

"You're not on a case?"

"A case of Scotch, maybe. Who'd hire me, Lieutenant?"

"That's the same question I asked."

"Well, you got your answer. Can I go now?"

"Just a second. Not so fast." His manner relaxed, and he sat down behind the desk, offered me a cigarette. I took it, and he lit it for me and then smiled.

"What you been doing, Cordell?" he asked.

"Spending my winters in Florida. Don't I look it?"

He seemed about to get sore, but then the smile flitted onto his face again, becoming a small chuckle in a few seconds. "Tell you the truth," he said abruptly, "I think you were right, Cordell. That bastard had it coming to him."

I didn't say anything. I watched his face warily.

"Fact," he went on, "you should have given him more. How'd you catch him, Cordell?"

"What do you mean?"

"What happened? The papers said you went into the bedroom and found him loving your wife? That right? What was the bastard doing?" His eyes were gleaming brightly now. "Was she really in a nightgown? Did he…"

I leaned over the desk and grabbed the lapels of his suit in both my hands. "Shut up!" I said. My face was tight and I was ready to tear this filthy weasel into little pieces.

"Listen, Cordell…" Some of his old manner was back, some of the hard shell of the policeman.

"Shut up!" I shoved him hard and he flew back into his chair, and then the chair toppled over and fell to the floor. He blinked his eyes, and all the filth in his mind crowded into his face, leaving a small man hiding behind the skirts of a big job. He scrambled to his knees and flicked open the bottom drawer of his desk. His hand crawled into the drawer like a fast spider.

He was pulling his hand out when I stepped behind the desk and kicked the drawer shut.

He would have screamed, but I kicked out again and this time it was where he lived, and he doubled up in pain, his face twisted into a horrible, distorted grimace.

I stood over him with my fists clenched. He'd forgotten all about the gun in the bottom drawer now. He had something more important to be concerned with.

"I'm leaving," I told him.

"You stinking…"

"You can send one of your boys after me if you like, Lieutenant. Unless you're afraid of walking down dark streets at night."

"You're not getting away with this," he gasped. "You're…"

"Assault and battery, resisting arrest…what else? I'll serve the sentence, Lieutenant, while you prepare your will."

"You threatening me, Cordell?"

I stood over him, and the look in my eyes told him I wasn't kidding. "Yes, Lieutenant, I'm threatening you. My advice is to forget all about this. Just forget I was even here."

He got to his feet and was about to say something when the door sprang open. The big cop, Jim, looked at the lieutenant and then at me.

"Everything all right, sir?" he asked.

Gunnisson hesitated a moment, and then his eyes met mine and he turned his face quickly. "Yes," he said sharply. "Goddamned chair fell over." He passed his hand over his scalp and said, "Show Mr. Cordell out. He was just leaving."

I smiled thinly, and Detective-Lieutenant Gunnisson picked up the chair and sat in it, busying himself with some reports on his desk. Jim closed the door behind him and I asked, "Did you really get a complaint?"

"Sure. What the hell you think—we got nothing better to do than play around with a monkey like you?"

I didn't answer him. I walked straight to the front door, down the front steps and out into the street.

Dusk crouched on the horizon, and then night sprang into its place, leaping into the sky like a black panther. The stars pressed inquisitive white noses against the black pane of darkness, and the moon beamed like a balding old man.

The neon flickers stabbed the darkness with lurid reds and greens, oranges, blues, giving spring her evening clothes. There was still a warm breeze in the air, and inside The Dewdrop I could hear a throaty tenor sax doing crazy things with *How High The Moon.*

It was ten o'clock.

I walked up the block quickly, the way a young girl anxious to meet her lover would walk. My heels clicked on the pavement, echoing in the darkness of the tree-lined street. I turned left on Burke, reached the elevated structure, took the steps up two at a time. I walked to the change booth, slipped a quarter under the grilled panel.

"What time's the next downtown train pull in?" I asked the attendant.

He glanced up at the clock. "About ten-oh-nine."

"Thanks," I said. I collected my change, shoved my way through the turnstile. The clock on the wall said ten-oh-six. I climbed the steps to the Downtown side. I reached the platform and waited, and in a few minutes a downtown express pulled in. The doors slid open, and I stepped into the train, starting to look immediately for a conductor. I was going to take a narrow gamble, and even if it paid off I didn't know where to go from there. But the gamble was necessary because so far I'd slammed into blank wall after blank wall—and Freddie was still loose somewhere in the city.

I found the conductor in one of the middle cars reading a morning newspaper. I sat down next to him and he glanced at me sideways and then went back to the paper.

"Are you the only conductor on the train?" I asked.

He looked up suspiciously. "Yes. Why?"

"Have you had the night shift long?"

"Past month. Why?"

The train rumbled into the Allerton Avenue station, and he got up to press the buttons that would open the doors. He stood between the cars, waiting for the passengers to load and unload, and then he came back to his seat.

"Why?" he asked immediately.

I fished the picture out of my jacket pocket. "Know this girl?"

He stared at the picture curiously, and then looked at me as if I were nuts. "Can't say that I do."

"Look at it hard," I said. "Look at it damned hard. She got on at Burke Avenue two or three times during the week. She always caught this train. Look at the goddamned picture!"

He looked at the picture hard, and the train rumbled toward the next station. He still hadn't said a word when we pulled into Pelham Parkway and he got up to press his buttons again. When he came back, he continued to look at the picture.

"We'll be in Grand Central before you make up your mind."

"I already made up my mind. I never seen her before." He paused. "Why do you want her?"

"Look at it again," I told him, almost reaching out for his throat. "She was a happy sort of kid. Smiling all the time. God-damn it, mister, remember!"

"There's nothing to remember. I just never seen her before."

I slapped the picture against the palm of my hand. "Jesus! Who else works on this train?"

"Just me and the motorman, that's all."

"Where's the motorman? First car?"

"Listen, you can't bother him with that…"

"Open your doors, mister. Here's Bronx Park East."

He turned to say something, then realized the train was already in the station. I left him as he stepped between the cars, and I ran all the way to the first car. I was wild now, reaching for straws, but someone had to remember—someone! The train was just starting up again when I reached the motorman's little compartment and yanked open the door.

He was a small man with glasses, and he almost leaped out of the window when I jabbed the picture at him.

"Do you know this girl?"

"*What!*"

"Look at this picture! Do you know this girl? Have you ever seen her before, riding on this train?"

"Hey!" he said, "you ain't allowed in here."

"Shut up and look at this picture."

He glanced at it quickly, switching his eyes back to the track ahead almost instantly. "No, I don't know her."

"You never…"

"I watch the tracks," he said dutifully, "not the broads that get on and off.…"

I slammed the door on his soliloquy and started toward the back of the train again. I was ready to beat the old man's head against the metal floor if he didn't start remembering damned soon. When I reached him, he shouted, "You get off this train! You get off this train or I'll get help at the next station."

I took a quick evaluation of his chances of ever remembering Betty, and when the train pulled into 180th Street I got off with the conductor swearing behind me. I crossed under the platforms and came up on the Uptown side. Then I took the next train back to Burke Avenue.

There were three cabs parked in the hack stand. I showed Betty's picture to each of the three drivers. None of them recognized her.

It was like a big merry-go-round with me grabbing at the brass ring and always missing. I was ready to call it quits again, ready to chuck the whole stinking mess back into Rudy's lap. But there was one person I wanted to see again. She'd given me almost everything I knew about Betty Richards, and I had a hunch I could get more information from her if I really tried.

I hoped she'd be at The Dewdrop, and I was happy to see her behind the counter when I walked in. The jukebox was bashing out some rock 'n' roll masterpiece, and the place was packed with teenaged boys and girls. I walked over to Donna and said, "Dance?"

She looked up and gave me a half-smile. "You still haven't shaved, have you?"

"No, I haven't."

The smile widened.

"Have you got a minute?" she said.

"Lots of them."

"It's time I had a cigarette break. Meet me outside, will you?"

She walked over to the owner of the joint, the guy with the mustache. He didn't seem too happy about her leaving him alone with the rock 'n' rollers. I watched through the plate-glass window as he pulled a sour face. And then, like most bosses, he let her go anyway. She was lighting a cigarette as she stepped outside. She leaned against the brick wall of the next-door building and said, "Phew!" She blew out a stream of smoke.

"I'm glad you, came, Matt," she said. "Those kids were beginning to get in my hair."

I blinked at the darkness. "I really came to ask more questions," I said.

"I don't care why you're here. You're here, that's all that counts."

We were quiet again until she asked, "Are you any closer to him?"

"Not really," I said. "I wanted to ask you more about him. Did she ever say anything that would…"

"Nothing, Matt. She talked about him like…well, you know how kids are. As if he were a knight or something. You know. She talked to me a lot. We hit it off right from the beginning. Those things happen sometimes."

"Yeah," I said. Donna knew nothing more about Freddie. Nothing.

This was the end of the trail. Curtain. Freddie was still a blank face with the hands of a strangler. Nothing more. I was ready to call it quits.

"I went over to her because she looked kind of lonely the first night she came in. We got to chatting and before the night was over we'd exchanged phone numbers. Never used them, but…"

"You still have the number?"

"Why, yes. I think so. Somewhere in my purse. She wrote it on a napkin."

"You'd better let me have it," I said. That was the coward's way of doing it. I'd call Rudy and break it to him over the phone. Tell him I'd done my damnedest but I was tired and beaten, and the police would have to do the rest.

Donna sighed. "Now? I thought we might…"

"Now," I said.

"I'll be right back."

She walked into the rectangle of light cast by the open door of the store and then stepped inside. She was back in a few minutes with her purse and the napkin. "Here it is. You're not going, are you?"

"I have to make a call."

"This is getting to be a habit, I know, but come back, Matt. This time I mean it. Please come back."

"You didn't mean it last time?"

She shrugged and smiled wistfully. "You know how it is. Come back to me, Matt. Come back."

I left her standing in the amber rectangle of light, and I walked to the nearest candy store and settled myself in the booth. I looked at the numbers written on the napkin with a ballpoint pen, and then began to dial. Halfway through, it occurred to me that Rudy wouldn't be home, not if he left for work at four-thirty in the afternoon. I finished dialing anyway, looking down at the scrawled numbers.

And all at once it hit, just like that, and I hung up quickly.

It made me a little sick, but it also made me feel a little better because it was all over now.

I was waiting for Freddie.

It was close to one-thirty in the morning, and the streets were deserted. Spring had retreated into a cold fog that clouded the lights from the lampposts and swirled underfoot like elusive ghosts.

I waited until he came around the corner of the big building, carrying his flashlight and his time clock. I listened to the clack of his heels against the sidewalk. The fog lifted a misty barrier between us, and he didn't see me until he was almost on me.

"Hello, Freddie," I said.

"Wh…" He stared at me.

He backed away a few paces, and his hand went to his mouth. He recognized me then, blinked his eyes several times, and said, "Matt. What are you doing here at this hour?"

"Waiting. Waiting for you."

"Matt…"

"You're a son of a bitch, Rudy," I said.

"Matt…"

"She looked just the way your wife did at that age, didn't she, Rudy? Isn't that what you told me?"

"Matt, you've got this all wrong."

"I've got it all right, Rudy. Why didn't you leave her alone? Why couldn't you leave her alone, you bastard?"

"Matt, listen to me…"

"Why'd you hire me? Because you knew I was a stumble-bum? Because your wife was hounding hell out of you to get a detective? Because you figured Matt Cordell was a drunkard who couldn't solve his way out of a pay toilet? Is that why?"

"No, Matt. I came to you because…"

"Shut up, Rudy! Shut your filthy mouth before I close it for good. You didn't have to kill her."

He crumbled then. He leaned back against the wall, and his face slowly came apart. He raised a trembling hand to his mouth. His teeth chattered.

"What happened?" I asked. "Was she finally going to talk? Was she finally going to tell all about her mysterious lover? Was that it?"

Rudy closed his eyes, nodding.

"So you killed her. Snuffed her out, and then drove to Yonkers and dumped her there."

"Stop it, Matt. Stop it! Please."

"I'd never have found Freddie, Rudy. Never. But a friend of

Betty's gave me something in her handwriting, and I remembered something you'd showed me a while ago. The address of
The Dewdrop, written in the same hand. And then I wondered
why Betty had given you the address—and then I thought about
your working hours and the time she always left the store. And
then I realized why a seventeen-year-old kid was so anxious to
keep her boyfriend a secret. Why'd she give you the address,
Rudy? Why?"

"She…she wanted me to…pick her up there at first. This
was after it had started…after our first time…after the first
time we knew we were in love. I told her it was dangerous, but
she gave me the address and we tried it a…a few times. Then I
suggested that she meet me here at the warehouse. We…we
used to go inside…Matt, don't look at me that way. I loved her.
Matt."

"Sure. You loved her enough to kill her. And you loved her
enough to hire a wino to find Freddie. Freddie—a nice code
name. A convenient tag in case the kid wanted to talk about her
friend." I bit down on my lip. "Was it you who sicked the cops
on me? Did I scare you when I came up with the code name?"

"I…I called the cops. I told them you were practicing ille-
gally."

"You did it wrong, Rudy."

"How could I tell my wife?" he said. "What could I do, Matt?
Betty was ready to crack, ready to tell all of it. Matt, Matt, I had
to. I…I used my hands. I…I did it without thinking. She…I
just…" He stopped, and his voice broke, and suddenly he was
crying. The fog swept in around us.

"What am I going to tell Madeline, Matt? What can I tell her?"

"She's your wife," I said.

He gripped my arms. "You tell her, Matt," he pleaded. The
tears rolled down his face, and he kept repeating "please" until
I shook his hands from my arms.

"Sure," I said. "Sure."

I brought Rudy to Detective-Lieutenant Gunnisson, and I left fast. Then bought a quart of wine, and I killed the whole goddamned thing before I worked up enough nerve to call Madeline and tell her about her husband.

It was hard.

And then I went home, and Madeline's sobs were in my ears for a long time before I finally drank myself to sleep.